MW01136738

FAUSTIAN FUTURIST

This book is dedicated to
Professor Gerald Feinberg (1933–1992),
my teacher, mentor, and friend.

FAUSTIAN FUTURIST

JASON REZA JORJANI

ARKTOS
LONDON 2020

Copyright © 2020 by Arktos Media Ltd.

All rights reserved. No part of this book may be reproduced or utilised in any form or by any means (whether electronic or mechanical), including photocopying, recording or by any information storage and retrieval system, without permission in writing from the publisher.

ISBN   978-1-912975-94-5 (Paperback)
                    978-1-912975-95-2 (Hardback)
                    978-1-912975-96-9 (Ebook)

COVER & LAYOUT Tor Westman

🌐 Arktos.com   f fb.com/Arktos   🐦 @arktosmedia   📷 arktosmedia

CONTENTS

"Vade retro Satanas!"

Something my uncle once said to me.

❧

"Abandon all hope, ye who enter here."

The quote from Dante's *Inferno* that I inscribed over the
entrance to my laboratory at Colorado Springs.

NEW SWABIA, ANTARCTICA 10,500 BC

Starved, naked, broken, they stood in chain gangs all across the mountainside and farmlands. One might have known that they were Semitic in appearance, if their heads had not been completely shaven, and their faces and bodies painted in a paste of chalk and sweat. Fear, black fear, pierced their flesh and bones like a substance, pervading every organ and aching cavity with a tender trembling. Time, for them, existed only in breaths. In, Out. In, Out. A struggle between survival and despair.

It would be a stretch to call these *things* 'human beings.' Not an ounce of dignity was left to them. In this land without night and day, their lives were an incomprehensible rush of grueling labor, followed in turn by a black coma of exhaustion that for some slipped seamlessly into death — which meant simply *freedom* — freedom from fear of miserable suffering, from fear of that dreaded and empty word "tomorrow."

Once in a while there were nightmares, usually a single paralyzing image: fallen beneath the shadow of that wrinkled countenance darker than death, staring down harder than an angry gorilla… the blinding flash of the harsh sun on the point of a descending spear…

a blood spattered, black leather boot on the chalky earth of the stone quarries.

The chains rattled to the ball when they fell, to the left and to the right. The Guardians walked up and down the lines vigilantly, pulling on the chains here and there, pealing this one and that one up off the face of the earth to be battered across the skull with the butt of a spear. Still, so many lay writhing like maggots. Some half alive, the corpses of others already rotting in the oppressive heat.

Glimpsing the sight of the Atlantean Guardsmen as they moved among the corpses, skewering them and clearing them to the side, would leave one with no doubt that these warriors were the most fearsome creatures that ever walked the face of the Earth. Proud and noble Africans with skin so purely black, blacker than black, that in the merciless sunshine of this bleached land they took on the indigo hue of blue corn. They had the features of their Nubian descendants, but they were colossally built, broad enough to bear the burden of their heaving muscles. It was almost as if their faces were incapable of showing joy, boredom, or anxiety. Rather, their rugged features were locked in absolutely fearless determination. One pitiless gaze from their small, darting eyes, set beneath an ever-wincing brow and fore-head wrinkled with anger, was enough to turn the hot beating heart of the common man to solid ice.

At the end of the line, just as all throughout it, there stood such a man. One of his herd. His nose broken and his ears boxed in. His head hung down, utterly demoralized, as his naked body flexed to heave the pick over his head and into the face of the stone cliff. Once, twice… Then it happened. He seemed to forget where he was, to forget the Guardsman towering over him. He seemed unable to remember for the life of him who he was, or what he was doing here. It was hot. That's all he knew. The sun beat down. He stopped and time slurred as he forgot to keep breathing. Sinking to his knees, slowly, he raised his eyes… A herd of Mammoths thundered across the distant plains slothfully, oblivious.

A kick in the head and he was back down in the dust. He could see the Guardsmen looming over him. The sun shone across their armor. Their fearsome countenances were framed, it seemed almost inseparably incased, in a crème colored metallic helmet that was rounded over the top of the head and overset with a raised "U" shaped symbol. It widened as it descended beneath a ridge in sharp angular planes to cover the back of the head, the ears, and it ended in a rigid protrusion (like the lower half of an octagon) around the jaw. Their shoulders, from the upper arms to their sunken and strained necks, were covered in massive iron pads, angular on the sides facing the chest, curved around the outward-facing shoulder and embossed in two layers. Their chests were brutally bare. Beneath their sculpted abs they wore a thick metal belt lined with a single firearm holster and other small weapons, like knives or grenades. Under the belt hung sheets of armor in tiers that covered the groin, buttocks, thighs and went all the way down to the knees, but was open at the sides, up to the hips.

Their gruff voices could bark orders and their spears could point until doomsday, but he would not get up this time. He just stared straight into the pure blue sky, as if he were trying to say with his eyes the words that he could not form with his mouth. As if he were trying to testify to its emptiness. He had forgotten that he was alive. Dust sprinkled down into his parched mouth as a boot impounded the odd number of teeth in his gaping jaws, stamping out a human face with the seal of eternity.

The ethereal Antarctic sun really set only once in many months. Nevertheless, the Guardsman seemed to know when it was time to head back toward the cyclopean walls of Atlantis. That is, the first ring of walls. There were three. Slaves were not even allowed past the first, except for domestic servants — who needed permits. On the treacherous mountain path, as far as their eyes could see, lining the way before them and behind, were planted the spears of Guardsmen crowned by human skulls. The miserable souls had to stare them in the face as they walked to the quarries every 'morning.' An affirmation of destiny, it would seem.

Spears moved among spears as the Guardsmen marched alongside the chain-gang, prodding it forward. Despite all the sophisticated gadgetry of their helmets and utility belts, each Guardsman carried without fail at his side a tall spear with a massive iron point and used it most efficiently of all his weapons — especially to gesture directions as he barked orders while keeping an imposing distance. It was better to keep one's distance from a Guardsman. For all but the slave, proximity was equated with certain death. The slave, who hobbled about amidst their boots, was already dead. Only the Atlantean Lords and Ladies could lock eyes with them, as a ringmaster gazes into the eyes of a mesmerized panther.

The Guardsmen coldly studied the lines of skulls, as if they read in them a symbolic revelation regarding mortality. Some of these skulls — spiked at an angle — seemed to look up defiantly through the hollows of their eye sockets, cursing the Sun as it circumnavigated the pole, again and again, marking out a great symbol of futility.

CHAPTER 1

STOLEN CHILD

They said they were my aunt and uncle. I always had my doubts. You see my mother was the black sheep of her family. They more or less disowned her after she married my father. (At least, that is the story they later told me.) So by the age of five, when it happened, I had never met her twin sister. She and my mother were identical twins, and that was a real mind fuck when they came to pick me up. There was a much older man with her, and this was supposed to be my uncle. He was heavyset and expensively dressed, but in the gaudy style of a gangster. My mother's doppelganger wore more elegant attire, including a fur coat that she wrapped me up in as she carried me to the car. This 'uncle' had tried to pick me up, but I looked at him mistrustfully and he backed off with an expression on his face that hinted that my mistrust was more than justified and would be longstanding. In fact, I was so ill at ease with him that I almost wanted to stay with the police. But my aunt, Nikita, knelt down and implored me to come with them.

They drove me from Brighton Beach to their apartment in Manhattan. It was a luxurious Penthouse in a high-rise building on the Upper East Side, which had a guestroom that was slowly converted into my new bedroom. That fall night, as I lay in a strange bed stiff as a log, with the lights on and my eyes wide open, all I could see were the horrific images playing themselves out over and over again. My mother pleading with my father to stop beating her. My little hand reaching for the steak knife on the kitchen counter to threaten him with it, so that I could protect her. His calloused hand easily twisting the knife out of mine, and then carving her up with it.

I was so hysterical with a tangle of overpowering fear, shock, and rage that it is hard to know how long I was screaming and weeping over my mother's mangled and bloody corpse while he paced the room frantically — cursing under his breath, pounding his forehead, and occasionally shouting at me. The next thing I remember is that wiry man in his blood-smeared wife-beater disappearing into their bedroom and then coming back with a pistol, which he proceeded to put in his mouth so that he could blow his brains out onto the stained and cracking wallpaper of our little living room.

They say that after suffering trauma a person sometimes succumbs to a deep sleep and then awakes with amnesia, both of the incident and of events leading up to it. That is not what happened to me. Nothing of my last day with my mother was lost to me. She had taken me to the local Orthodox Church, where I always loved seeing her light the red glass candles under the glowing gold-leaf of the Russian icons. Then we walked along the beach from Brighton to Coney Island, where she took me to ride on the Wonder Wheel. I'll never forget her face, look- ing out over the heaving Atlantic Ocean, on that cold grey day. There was an impenetrably profound sadness in her eyes, especially when she looked at me. For someone who was only 33 years of age, there was so much sadness, guilt, and regret in that gaze. It was as if she was apologizing to me from the depth of her being for who knows what.

Perhaps I was staying so wide awake because, on some uncon- scious level, I was protecting myself from forgetting – guarding myself against the possibility that I might protect myself *by* forgetting. Or maybe that is exactly what would have happened if I had just lain there long enough into the morning to be exhausted. But not long after the sun started pouring in through the blinds, I heard my uncle grumble a few words to my aunt in Russian and then slam the door shut on his way to work. Never in all the years that I lived with them did it become clear to me exactly what this 'work' consisted of. It was only much later (relative to my brief life) that I was able to make a few educated guesses.

In any case, I might have finally fallen asleep after he left, but my aunt came into what was then still the guestroom and could tell that I had been awake all through the night. First she laid down next to me, and ran her fingernails through my hair in that hypnotic way that would become customary. But when this did not put me to sleep either, and she noticed that my clothes stank of the dried sweat with which they were saturated, she took my hand and brought me over to the bathroom in the master bedroom. It had a window facing the rising sun and I vividly recall the morning light illuminating the white tile floor.

She explained that there was no need to go back for my clothes, or for that matter, any of my things "in that awful house." Uncle would get me new clothes, and whatever else I wanted. He was going to bring some back 'home' with him after work today. Meanwhile, I could wear one of his t-shirts after I got out of the bath. She explained this to me as she filled the tub and pulled the clothes off my listless body. Then my aunt, who acted as if she did not want to let me out of her sight, slipped her silk pajamas off before stepping into the bathtub with me.

Her body was also like my mother's, but without all the bruises and somehow less worn down. Her breasts were just as small, but they seemed more firm, and the nipples were much larger — or maybe I just never remember having seen my mother with hard nipples. She certainly wasn't as thin. In fact, my aunt had a potbelly. As she stepped in over me, I could also tell that my aunt's hair was naturally the same dark brown color as my mother's, she had just died it platinum blond — I mean on her head. It was striking when taken together with her green eyes. She shampooed and soaped me, and then sat there quietly in the sunlight for a long while, holding my body between her strong thighs with her arms wrapped around me and her elbows resting on her bent knees. The sunlight streamed through the steam from the warm water. It was unreal. Mesmerizing. She would occasionally whisper into my ear in a tongue that sounded similar to the Russian that I was familiar with, but not enough to really understand it.

It was only years later, after the death of my uncle, that she confessed that the language (which she never spoke in front of him) was Ukrainian. She admitted that my mother was not really a Russian, but a Ukrainian, and that they had been born near Crimea in a coastal town on the Black Sea. It was only then that I grasped why I could not make out my mother's words in that last terrible fight as she yelled imploringly at my father. I had assumed that the traumatic shock of the event occulted their meaning, but she was actually speaking Ukrainian. Was my father, then, also a Ukrainian?

My aunt did not want to talk about my father, but once, when she was even more drunk than usual and we were alone together, she told me that what uncle had said all of these years about my father being a Russian communist was a lie. It was true that he had been investigated by McCarthy and the FBI, whose men in black suits I vaguely remember showing up to our home. But, my aunt explained, father misled them into suspecting him. He was indeed Ukrainian, and most certainly not a communist, let alone a KGB agent. There was an enigmatically fierce pride in her eyes when she said this.

Let me not get ahead of myself. When my uncle came home that evening and saw me in his shirt, which went down to my knees, he laughed. It was one of the few times I would ever hear him laugh, except for when he was drinking vodka with his friends and they would all burst out loudly laughing together. He brought me back some new clothes, and these were eventually replaced with ones that fit better. I remember the awkward experience of shopping with my aunt. Everyone assumed that she was my mother, and then wondered about how strange our interactions were. Neither of us ever corrected them.

School was another matter. The teachers and the principal treated me differently from the other children. I suppose they had been told what happened. It was difficult to make friends. The bus rides from Manhattan up to Horace Mann in Riverdale were long and lonely.

My room started to fill up and really become mine, rather than a guestroom. I remember laying on the carpeted floor and reading comic books. My favorites were the *X-Men* and *Batman*. I especially identified with Bruce Wayne, for obvious reasons. The noir crime atmosphere of the *Detective Comics* in which Batman was featured also appealed to me. You see, after a while, my aunt started letting me watch *The Naked City* with her on television. It was a film-noir style crime and detective series set right here in New York City. I think she realized that instead of triggering traumatic memories in a debilitating way, watching a show like that, even at such a young age, would help me to process what happened and make me feel like such terrible crimes were a part of life and I wasn't so singled out. Well, at any rate, that's what I told myself about why she let me watch it. As a kid, I wanted to be a detective. Our school's motto appealed to me, *Magna est veritas et praevalet* — "Great is the truth and it prevails."

For a long time, I also thought that hunger for truth was what motivated my intense interest in mathematics and science. I excelled in those subjects. To be frank, I was an all-around excellent student, and my near-photographic memory made History and Literature easy for me, but at a young age I was especially enthusiastic about math, chemistry, and biology. No one who knew me as a child would have been surprised that I eventually got an undergraduate degree in Physics. I wrote that I *thought* truth-seeking was what motivated me. Eventually, I realized that my enthusiasm for the stable and hard certainties of math and of the more mathematical sciences was a psychological defense against the almost overwhelming chaos of the uncanny and downright bizarre experiences that filled my life.

It started with the recurring dreams. No, these were not nightmares rehashing the death of my parents. I had surprisingly few of those. I am talking about a series of dreams that I started having around the age of six, where I was an old man living out of suitcases in hotel rooms. Although I couldn't call them nightmares, they were extremely disturbing. I would wake up from them filled with the most profound sadness, a feeling of being forlorn that did not belong to the consciousness of a six year old (however tragic his life had been thus far). No, the inner life of that old man would bleed over into my waking consciousness for a while after each dream.

He had been abandoned and forgotten by the world. I saw him in a place that I later identified as Bryant Park, feeding pigeons, who were his only friends. How is it possible for a six year old to know what it feels like for an old man to pull the loose skin tighter on his face as he shaves in his bathroom mirror? Or what it feels like to pull your suit pants up too high, and buckle them too tight with your belt, because you're starving yourself to death, and although your clothes are all too loose you can't afford to buy new ones. How does a six or seven year old know what that feels like? I did. The lobby of the hotel he was living in had high ceilings, and I remember him sitting there in a chair, with a filthy spittoon next to it. What little he ate, he ate in the diner that was connected to that lobby. He couldn't walk far and had a limp. You see he had been hit by the front grills of one of those old New York checkered cabs, and it had fractured his leg. But when bystanders rushed to the old man's aid, he refused treatment. He was too embarrassed to wind up in a hospital and have the doctors leak to the press that the great man he once was had fallen on such hard times that he couldn't pay the hospital bill. Later in life, I recognized the hotel. It was the New Yorker.

My strange childhood experiences were by no means limited to these recurring dreams. Some of them are *so* strange that I cannot for the life of me put them into any sensible context. I am sure that, given my history, most psychologists would consider them false memories. But they are not. These things happened, and were as 'real' as anything that happens. Let me give you just a few examples.

Once, my aunt took me to a house that had been decorated to look like the North Pole — you know, the way a place might be done up like that around Christmas. Except it wasn't Christmas, and the snow in the yard was fake. In fact, it was summer! She told me that we were going to see Santa Claus. We went up this narrow stairway in the house, which was full of dolls of elves and lit up candy canes and the like. One of the doors in the hallway upstairs was marked with a sign that read "Santa Claus" in childlike handwriting. It was creaked open, and I can't remember a thing that happened after we walked into it, other than that I had every intention of sitting on Santa's lap. Oh, one more thing. There was an ice cream truck parked in the lot out front. I recognized it as the same one from our neighborhood, because even though no one seemed to be inside, its music was going and this truck was broken and had a peculiar glitch in its tune.

Then there was this greyhound bus ride that we took. It was just my aunt and I. We were headed back from Shoreham, Long Island, where for some reason she had taken me to see a run down brick building that she said had been a mad scientist's laboratory. I guess I had become obsessed with the Frankenstein films, and she told me this man, who shared my name, "Nikolai", would create artificial lightning inside the lab, like the lightning that brought the monster to life in the movies. Or maybe she had another reason for taking me there, as I later came to suspect. But the building was practically a ruin, and being inside it, I was suddenly plunged into the densest depression that I have ever felt. But that is not what I wanted to recount.

We were headed back from this place, and just before we got on the bus, a shudder ran through my spine as I noticed a freakishly tall and very peculiar looking man in a black suit and black tie, wearing a fedora hat. In retrospect, I would say he looked a bit like Lurch from the Adams Family. He was essentially Nordic in appearance, with buzz-cut platinum blond hair, but his facial features were extremely chiseled with high cheekbones and preternaturally large, mesmerizing blue eyes, sunken into deep sockets that surrounded them with dark shadows. The brim of his black hat appeared to conceal an unusually high forehead. He was loading what appeared to be a violin case into the luggage compartment under the bus. He hurled it with such force that the case popped open, and there inside it was the exsanguinated cadaver of a black dog, crushed in such a manner as to make it fit into the case. The man in black gave me a hard stare, one that silently said, "Yeah? What are you going to do about it?!" At this point my aunt, who appeared not to have noticed, was pulling me by the arm up the stairs of the bus. What is at least as odd, is that this man, did not join us as a passenger.

We had a ski house in Hunter Mountain, a couple of hours north of the city. My uncle had taught me to ski. Despite his weight, and his age, he was pretty damn good at skiing. One Friday evening, we were suppose to go up to the chalet for the weekend, but my uncle had some 'business' in the city that came up at the last minute. I was terribly disappointed. So instead of cancelling the trip, my aunt drove the two of us up there herself. I used to love watching her when she would drive. Bobby Darin's "Dream Lover" was playing on the radio as we wound our way through those narrow, wooded mountain passes with frozen waterfalls. Anyway, it was really late by the time we arrived. She quickly cooked us a little dinner from groceries that had been packed in the back of the car. Then we went to bed.

In the middle of the night, probably somewhere around 2am if I had to guess, my aunt came into my room and woke me up. She was crouched down by the side of the bed, fully dressed in her ski outfit, and put her long bony finger across her lips as if to say: "Shhh." She got me out of bed, dressed me warmly, and then took me out into the cold to hike up into the woods of the hillside overlooking the ski resort, under the crisp starry night sky. She held me with one arm around my shoulders, with my head pressing into her jacket, as the snow crunched under our boots.

We got to a little clearing on the wooded hillside where the snow was slightly brushed off of what appeared to be a wooden trap door.

Like a cellar door, with a black metal handle. She brushed some of the dusting of the freshest snow off it, and then threw it open. Her green eyes were sparkling at me mischievously, as if she were also a child and we were on an adventure together. The moonlight made the platinum hair falling over her shoulders shine so steely. She took my hand and we descended into the darkness, down some creaky old wooden steps until we felt packed earth beneath our feet. I could hear glass and metal clinking, and then the blue flame of the lamp that she had reached for in the darkness flickered on.

What I could see of the walls were covered in embossed designs, as if they were pressed into the earth, but baked hard. My child's mind could hardly make out what these depicted, but in retrospect I hazard that they were Gorgons and owls. The place smelled of something between sulfur and cinnamon. I could feel goose bumps on the back of my neck as I got the impression that we were being watched from out of the dark corners. You might imagine that at this point I would have been terrified. Perhaps, and there was certainly something of terror in the emotions that seized my whole body with a visceral intensity beyond the mind's feeble comprehension. But that terror was overpowered by an awful fascination and excitement as my aunt proceeded to take her clothes off. All of her clothes. She took mine off too, and pulled me down onto the cold packed earth with her. Her nipples were so hard, and so was I. She was dripping wet when I slipped into her.

The next thing I remember is her making breakfast in the morning. Now and then she cast me penetrating glances as I sat at the table while she was cooking in the kitchen. It was as if she was wondering whether I would let myself believe that it was just a dream. But I wouldn't, and at the first opportunity that I had to go out hiking into the woods alone — near sunset on some late afternoon a couple of years later — I went looking for the clearing and the trap door. I was ten years old. What a feeling of dread and anticipation filled me as I finally scraped the snow off the wood and found it. When I mustered the courage to pull the black metal handle, it broke off from being so badly rusted. I resolved to come back with a shovel, perhaps in the Spring, and pry it open. But my uncle died of a heart attack before the end of the ski season, and my aunt sold the Hunter Mountain house.

By now, I am sure that you see what I mean, and I have not even mentioned that sometimes I could hear people's thoughts in my head. It could easily have become debilitating. This also gave me a very early insight into how hypocritical most people are. It was especially bad when my uncle would invite people over for their boisterous parties. His macho friends contemptuously thought that I was an introvert crippled by shyness, but they did not realize that it sickened me to hear their thoughts — or feel their desires — inside my mind, especially since they all wanted to fuck my aunt. Well, she was beautiful, and so much younger than my uncle and most of his 'associates.' They wouldn't dare slight him by addressing her vulgarly around the dining table, but they were all imagining that they could show her a better time in bed. This 'ability' also got me into a lot of trouble at school. Kids are cruel enough to each other out loud, let alone in their heads.

So math and science really did become my salvation. I relished the reliability of equations and the elemental stability of nature's laws as I (falsely) imagined them. When I discovered Asimov's *Foundation* series, and read it voraciously, I realized to my delight that it might be possible to take the same approach toward Psychology and History. I started psychoanalyzing the literature we were assigned, trying to categorize the behavior of the protagonists under certain definite patterns of personality that would have predictive power. Far more troublesome, at least for my teachers, was an increasing insistence that there had to be laws of history as there were laws of nature. My memory was excellent, so none of my history teachers could fault me for having forgotten any of the names and dates that we were forced to mindlessly 'learn.' That made them all the more frustrated in the face of my incessant challenges to them to *explain* the history that we were being taught. In other words, to convey some understanding of *why* things happened where and when they did, what the logic, interconnection, and developmental trajectory of these events was supposed to be.

Given my Russian background, some of the faculty at posh Horace Mann started to suspect that I was raised and indoctrinated by Marxists. At the time, I had no idea that Karl Marx had sought to develop a science of history, not altogether unlike the Galactic "Psychohistorians" that Asimov had imagined in *Foundation*. Their casting of aspersions was a catalyst for my discovering Marx. It is a good thing that my uncle was dead, because I think if he had seen me come home with the school library's *Communist Manifesto* in hand he would have given me an unforgettable beating. "Like father, like son," he'd have said. Nikita was knowingly amused, and even bought me my own copy of the book. She always encouraged my intellectual development.

My serious interest in Marx, and then more generally in the claim of Communism to be a comprehensive science, served to enliven the connection that I had with my Russian heritage. Sputnik and the Soviet dominance in space only strengthened my pride in the Promethean spirit of the Communist commitment to science and technological innovation as the spearhead of human empowerment and liberation from every manner of backwardness and oppression. Senator McCarthy was, to my adolescent eyes, a modern day American inquisitor comparable to those who ordered witches to be burned alive at Salem. By the time that the Cuban Missile Crisis took place in the weeks before Halloween of 1962, I had already developed a strange sense of the Soviet Union as my motherland. I say "strange" because, although I did feel that natal and organic tie to Russia, it was the universality — even the *cosmic* destiny — of the Soviet idea that really appealed to me.

The 1964 release of *Dr. Strangelove* only intensified this feeling, and it probably triggered what would become an obsession with nuclear war. I remember reading Herman Kahn's book, *Thinking About The*

Unthinkable at the age of seventeen, only a couple of years after it came out. Kahn was a futurist and military strategist for the RAND Corporation think tank, and one of the founders of the Hudson Institute. He applied systems theory and game theory to thermonuclear warfare in what was the first, and what remains to this day, the most chilling and hair-raising analysis of how a nuclear war could be fought and 'won.' Kahn was one of several figures that inspired Stanley Kubrick's character of "Dr. Strangelove", specifically his earlier book *On Thermonuclear War,* and I admit that articles that noted this fact led me to *Thinking About The Unthinkable* and subsequent futurist writings of his, such as his visionary speculations on *The Year 2000.*

However fueled by news, films, and books my concern with nuclear war may have been, it was much more personal and profound than any morbid intellectual curiosity. I had nightmares. Literally. I would wake up in the middle of the night drenched in sweat, and then go out onto the wrap-around terrace of our Penthouse apartment, with its spherical lights, breathing the night air with such urgency that it was as if I had just been exhumed from a mass grave. I would survey the expansive panorama of the city lights framing the primal darkness of Central Park, and superimpose upon it the horrific sight witnessed in these recurring nightmares. They would begin with me in bed, waking suddenly from a blinding flash of light. Then I would go out onto the terrace through the shards of the glass doors shattered by a shockwave, only to see New York City burst into flames. The sensation of my body burning as if from within is what would wake me up. There were other thoughts in the dream, but these remained indistinct. It was as if they were the memories I had at the moment when I was awakened by the Soviet strike, memories of things that haven't happened yet. It would be a few years before I could tease apart what these 'memories' of the future consisted of and what picture they painted of the events leading to the war.

My aunt was in her mid-forties at the time, sleeping alone in the master bedroom, about a decade after my uncle's fatal heart attack and just before she died of her overdose. On one of the first occasions that I was visited by this nightmare of a nuclear holocaust, she heard me go out onto the terrace and joined me there. It was a hot summer night and she poured chilled Stolichnaya for us as she sat on the cushioned chairs in her silk robe, encouraging me to confide in her. I did, and she said some very strange things to me about atomic bombs and the aftermath of the Second World War that I did not understand until much later in my life. These things had to do with the Germans having built nuclear weapons *before* the Americans. She said that people, both Americans and Russians, had been told many lies about the war with Germany. This was the same night that she let it slip that my father was really Ukrainian, like herself and my mother, and that he was the furthest thing from a Communist, although he had behaved in such a manner as to deliberately come under the suspicion of having been one.

We got really drunk together that night. When I braced her as she eventually stumbled through the living room and the hallway back to bed, I was not of a mind to resist as she undid her robe and pulled me in with her by my hair. "*Pavuk plete,*" she whispered as her nails ran across my scalp and dug into the back of my neck, "*Pryyde pavuk.*" The spider is weaving. The spider will come.

I didn't know why at the time, but those cryptic words in my mother's tongue made me think of the *Mabuse* movies that my aunt had taken me to see with her. It was a trilogy of Fritz Lang, the last installment of which had come out in 1960, when she caught me up on re-releases of the first two films so that I could appreciate it. My mother's name, Marianna, was the Russian iteration of the name of the female lead, and the super-villain's lover, in *The Thousand Eyes of Dr. Mabuse*. That stuck with me. So did the concept of "The Empire of Crime" masterminded by the parapsychological terrorist whose spectre defies death and prosecution by any earthly law and order. Something about the way my aunt whispered "Spider" in Ukrainian that night made me think of Mabuse and his invisible Reich.

CHAPTER 2

PROJECT PROMETHEUS

The sun had just risen when, on an early September morning of 1965, I arrived on the campus of Columbia University well in advance of my first college class. The steps around Athena were still empty, so no one saw me kneel to "Alma Mater" before I ascended the grand stairway up to the Rotunda. Strolling back and forth along the colonnade, I looked over the shoulders of the goddess of Wisdom and War and surveyed the august names engraved above its Ionic columns, with Plato, Milton, and Goethe, among them. Philosophy fascinated me, and I was drawn to Luciferian or Faustian literature, but I had already decided to exploit my aptitude for mathematics and exact sciences by majoring in Physics.

The fact that I did not live on campus meant that I was less distracted from my studies. I would commute daily from 77th and Cherokee, essentially spanning Manhattan every morning in a pilgrimage from the East River to the Hudson. I would often take the time to walk to the bank of each of them, so that I could overlook both on the same day. After my aunt died of a drug overdose (no doubt exacerbated by her consumption of alcohol), I decided to stay in our apartment. Somewhat morbidly, I even moved into the master bedroom and slept in the bed that I found her lifeless body sprawled across one morning in the late summer before my first year of college. The doormen, handymen, and the management were a bit unnerved by this, and there were undoubtedly unkind rumors circulating about me. But my aunt had left me the apartment in her will, together with everything that she inherited after my uncle died. This inheritance amounted to a small fortune.

One might imagine that, being independently wealthy, I would have used my Penthouse apartment for wild college parties. Actually, the wealth somehow served to increase my isolation. So did the fact that everything in our building was self-contained. We had our own bank, post office, grocery store, shopping mall, full dry cleaning service, and other amenities catering to shut-ins who liked to pretend to be "too busy" to see to all these things by themselves. Truth be told, this is one of the reasons that I stayed. There was even a regularly scheduled private bus to shuttle residents to midtown Manhattan and back home, so that we could avoid crowds on the Subway. I would often walk to and from Columbia, across Central Park. That helped to keep me in shape, with little other exercise left in my life. After my aunt died, the thought of going skiing alone in the winters was depressing to me. The two of us had continued to go up to Hunter Mountain together even after she sold the ski house. We would stay at Scribner Hollow, and would often be the last ones soaking in the underground grotto at night. It was almost inconceivable for me to go back there without her. Besides, I had never learned to drive and that would make it hard to stay overnight.

For my first few years at Columbia, that is, before the events that transpired on the campus during my senior year in 1968, the closest rapport that I had with anyone was not with a fellow student, but with a teacher. After taking several classes with him, I became the protégé of Professor Gerald Feinberg of the Physics Department. Gary was a dynamic lecturer with a dazzling ability to convey complex theoretical knowledge in a way that could even be compelling to laymen. He would go on to make a career out of writing books that popularized the promise of science and technology for transforming the human future. Gary had penetrating and mischievous eyes that reflected his visionary genius, but for such a farsighted man he was also exceptionally kind and patient. By the time I was writing my senior thesis paper on the Many-Worlds Interpretation of Quantum Mechanics under his advisement, he had become my friend and not just my teacher. Gary had me over for dinner at his home on more than one occasion. We would often have coffee together around Morningside Heights, especially at his favorite Hungarian Pastry Shop across from the Cathedral of St. John.

My thesis already marked a transition from Physics into Philosophy, and if a less philosophically-minded Professor than Gary Feinberg had been my adviser, I doubt that it would have been approved. Not only did Gary approve my thesis, he urged me to take a few more philosophy courses, stay an extra year at Columbia—a decision that would prove fateful—and secure a second major, in Philosophy, before graduating in 1969. My thesis argued that the MWI of Hugh Everett was incoherent because it denied free will, which is the precondition of even the most basic intentionality required to frame *any* testable theoretical model of physical phenomena.

Basically, the idea was that if the quantum uncertainty of probability functions was resolved *in every way that it could possibly be*, but that this was hidden from us because each resolution of a wave into a discrete and measurable particle took place in one of infinitely many parallel universes that are *isolated from one another*, then no 'person' in any one of these universes—including ours—ever really made a choice about anything. If our brains are made up of quantum particles, then what seem to be our trains of thought, let alone our decisions, are actually just the random outcome of wave function collapses. In every one of the parallel universes where there is a version of us, each of us thinks everything imaginable and makes every 'decision' leading to every action that we do not 'choose' to do in the other universes—including this one.

The moral implications of this are monstrous, but even just on an intellectual level, it makes nonsense out of rational thought. The kind of reasoning involved in developing a scientific theory, which must be testable in practice, in other words, through meaningful action, is a cognitive process that is intrinsically intentional. It requires some basic level of free will, even if this will is massively conditioned by all kinds of contingencies – physical, biological, psychological — beyond our control. It still has to be the case that the scientist has some cohesive agency, which is impossible unless he has an individual character defined by a coherent trajectory of meaningful choices that reflect *his* persona, aims, and interests. That kind of agency is precluded by the MWI of Quantum Mechanics, and so the theory itself is incoherent because it denies the ontological or epistemological preconditions of *any* meaningful scientific thought *as such*.

Far more interesting than this thesis, is what came out of it in terms of my relationship with Gary. Feinberg found the paper fascinating for two reasons that were very relevant to his own work. The first was that it considered the scientist as a *type* of person and science as an *activity* in humanistic terms or from a perspective that I later realized was "existential." Feinberg was hardly an existentialist, but at just that time he had been developing a Promethean vision of the social task of the scientist to expand and explore the horizon of the human potential for future evolution. The second thing about my senior thesis that appealed to him was its implicitly non-reductionist view of the relationship between consciousness and physical phenomena. My argument at least implied that we needed a new Physics that, even if it did not abandon materialism altogether, would allow for an account of human thought and intentional action that described the mind as something more than an epiphenomenon of physical mechanisms. Gary was also looking for this, and had been so bold as to seriously consider Parapsychology research as a domain wherein he might find evidence for it.

Before coming to Columbia, Gary had been a member of the Institute of Advanced Study at Princeton University and garnered a security clearance at Brookhaven National Laboratory on Long Island. Only those closest to him knew that this had brought him within the orbit of private think tanks and secret policy advisement groups with access to classified projects. Later, these groups would also grant him entrée to Rockefeller University, where he worked part-time in addition to his teaching responsibilities at Columbia. This nexus of clandestine connections was the matrix for Gary's monumental 1967 paper in *Physical Review* on the "Possibility of Faster-Than-Light Particles" and his monumental 1969 book, *The Prometheus Project: Mankind's Search for Long-Range Goals*. The 1967 paper postulated the existence of a type of quantum particles that Feinberg named "tachyons", which he proposed were the physical basis for the hitherto anomalous mental abilities of precognition and psychokinesis. The 1969 book was nothing less than a proposal for a techno-scientific elite to take control of the world and guide a unified humanity into the achievement of Promethean goals such as radical life-extension (including by means of cryonics), the development of superhuman intelligence (by means of both genetic engineering and computational cybernetics), and colonization of the entire solar system. During the whole period in which Gary developed this vision, from 1966 through 1969, I was his protégé and confidant. Though I admit that in 1968 and 1969, my attention was more than a little divided.

Shortly before the Spring of 1968, after I had begun seriously pursuing my second major, in Philosophy, I met a woman studying at Barnard (which was Columbia University's girls college until coed integration in 1983). At that point I was almost 21. Anna was only 19. We met at the Hungarian Pastry Shop, where she was reading Dostoyevsky *in the original Russian*. This, together with her extraordinarily Eurasian beauty, was striking enough for me to overcome my characteristic introversion and address her *in Russian*. I asked, "Was Raskolnikov wrong to think he sinned by aspiring to be a Superman?"

She was toward the end of *Crime and Punishment*, and besides by the looks of it she had read the beat up volume several times already. To my extremely inappropriate question, forwarded without any pleasantries or personal introduction, she replied in a slow and deliberate manner, after only a brief silence during the course of which she looked unflinchingly into my eyes, I dare say even trying to pry into my soul. "He was mistaken about what it means to be a Superman. Wrong about it when he aspired to be one, and even more so, when he repented of it."

Within days of that first encounter Anna and I were taking the Subway from her dorm at the top of the hill on Morningside Heights down to the Village to see late night screenings of Russian cinema together. One of our favorite places became the Nicholas Roerich Museum on West 107th Street, across from Riverside Drive. She introduced me to a subversive group of Russian thinkers and writers who had been exiled, mostly to Paris, after the 1917 revolution. My aunt had mentioned some of these philosophers, but it was only after I met Anna that I read them. The two with whom I felt the greatest affinity were Nikolai Berdyaev and Konstantin Tsiolkovsky. The former was an existentialist whose fundamental concern was with the idea of freedom and its realization as a divine destiny. The latter, who was the only one of this group of dissidents to evade exile, was a rocket scientist and futurist. He advocated our eugenic evolution into psychic cosmonauts who would leave Earth behind as a womb while colonizing the universe; the Soviets overlooked his ideological deviation, especially his eugenicist views, so that he could set up their rocketry program.

Despite her intense metaphysical idealism and romantic orientation toward life, or perhaps *because* of it, Anna was also radically political. She belonged to the Students for a Democratic Society (SDS) on campus, although she often clashed with the other members over their materialism. She envisioned a convergence of two future revolutions, one in America toward sociopolitical Communism, and one in Russia away from putatively 'scientific' materialism and back to the eclectic mysticism so characteristic of the Eurasian soul. Anna believed that catalyzing and alchemically fusing these two revolutions was the only way to save the world from nuclear Armageddon. This idea resonated deeply with me and, for the tragically brief time that we were together, I embraced it as my own mission. What I brought to this mission was my scientific mind. I prevailed upon her that the problem with the Soviet Union was not its valorization of science, but a false reduction of scientific exploration to a materialist and mechanistic dogma that was at least equally entrenched in America and the West at large. The 1970 publication of *Psychic Discoveries Behind the Iron Curtain* went a long way toward convincing her of this. As it turned out, the Soviet Union was more open to Parapsychology, or "Psychotronics" research as they called it, than the American scientific establishment. The United States was forced to catch up. I will come, momentarily, to the significant role that I secretly played in this through my connection with Gary. But first, let me finish recounting how things unfolded with Anna, especially in those tumultuous years of 1968 and 1969 on the campus of Columbia University.

Anna introduced me to Mark Rudd and his inner circle, just before they led the student takeover of Columbia in late April of 1968. This group also included Ted Gold, who as it turned out would not have long to live. Anna and I visited Gold a number of times at his apartment on West 94th street, where I also met David Gilbert and Bob Feldman, who were living there as well. By the time the Communist red flag was raised over the Mathematics building on the student-occupied campus, I was recognizable to most of the core members of SDS who would go on to form the Weatherman underground cell in New York City. The one exception was Terry Robbins, who I did not get to know until the "collective" (as they liked to call it) relocated to the townhouse at 18 West 11th Street, which belonged to Cathy Wilkerson's father. You see, Cathy, and a number of other young white people who belonged to this group, actually came from money and were rebels against their rich parents. That fact put me somewhat at ease about dealing with them, although I *tried* to never invite any of these individuals back to my luxurious apartment on the Upper East Side.

In any case, Anna and I were there on campus during the seven day occupation of Columbia at the end of April of '68. Gary had only a vague sense that I was somehow involved with the SDS leaders of the takeover, but it was clear enough to him that he expressed his concern. When the NYPD stormed the campus with tear gas and cleared out the occupied buildings in the early morning of April 30th, Anna and I managed to slip out through a hidden tunnel system under the Physics building that Gary had told me about. It led to a sealed off part of the campus that was still radioactive from the research that had been done there in the early 1940s in order to develop the atomic bomb as part of the Manhattan Project. It was Columbia University's continuing relationship with the Military-Industrial Complex (and its war in Vietnam) that had triggered the student uprising in 1968. The "Gym Crow" plan to build a segregated gymnasium only acted as accelerant.

It was after we lost Columbia that SDS began to transform into the Weatherman organization. A lot of the restructuring took place in Chicago, under the leadership of Bernadine Dohrn and Bill Ayers. I only met Dohrn on a couple of occasions, although I admit that was quite enough for her to have been seared into my mind. She was a fiery raven, and quite unforgettable. Anna was not so deeply involved in SDS as to have been privy to any of the infighting that led to the splintering of the original broad-based student movement, and to the formation of Weatherman as the strongest of the breakaway groups. All we knew was that after whatever went down in Chicago, and following the failed occupation of the Columbia campus, the New York members of the group relocated their base of operations from Morningside Heights to Greenwich Village, a kind of shared campus for New York University and the New School for Social Research.

That is where my involvement with these terrorists intensified, partly on account of the fact that after I graduated from Columbia, I took my second major and used it to gain admittance to the New School in pursuit of a masters degree in Philosophy. I was a graduate student there when, on March 6, 1970, the Greenwich Village townhouse exploded because the nail bomb that Terry was building had faulty wiring. Ted Gold and Diana Oughton were killed together with Terry in the blast. The two Cathys, Boudin and Wilkerson, made it out of the wreckage alive. Dustin Hoffman, who lived next door, was there surveying the smoking ruins of the townhouse as I got the two of them into a taxi and fled from the crime scene to my apartment on 77th and Cherokee. It was the first time that I had let any Weather 'men' in there.

Kathy Boudin and Catherine Wilkerson were not unattractive women, Boudin especially so, with her dark hair and handsome features. Cathy Wilkerson's light brown, at times almost dirty blond, hair was less to my taste, but there was a beauty to the Nordic determination often seen in her face and I liked the bookish look that her glasses gave her. Of course, these had been broken in the blast that day. I took the two women in through the side entrance (the one toward Cherokee, not York Avenue) so that the doormen would be less likely to notice the dust covering their clothes and put two and two together when they watched the nightly news. All I needed was to lose this apartment, or likely much worse, for harboring fugitives caught in the act of preparing for a terrorist attack.

Anna met us there. I told her to bring some of her clothes for the two women to change into, including underwear. Both had soaked theirs through. By the time Anna let herself in with her set of keys they were standing in the bathtub of the master bedroom together, still dazed and in shock, using the removable shower head and my sponge to scrub the paste of piss and pulverized red brick off each other's thighs with their soiled panties strewn across the tile floor. Anna quickly snatched these up and threw them into the trash bin next to the toilet whose lid I was sitting on, talking to the two fugitives. I got up and motioned for her to sit in my place, but she declined and said she was going to go make a pot of coffee for the girls. I had an extra bathrobe that Anna would wear on the nights that we slept together here rather than at her cozy dorm in Morningside Heights. So one of the women was in my bathrobe and the other wore Anna's while they sat cross-legged sipping coffee on the King-sized bed, propped up by the bigger pillows on it. Anna and I sat on the two chairs that were in the bedroom, one of them belonging to my aunt's old makeup table.

That night was the only time that Anna and I ever participated in any of the habitual orgies of the Weather Underground. It was hardly a typical example of these loveless fuck-fests, which were meant to bond "comrades" together with the glue of erotic energy and sexual intimacy. From what I gathered, there was hardly anything truly erotic or intimate about the so-called "free love" in the "collective" whose Village love nest (and bomb factory) was now in smoldering ruins. It was all about proving oneself. I wonder how often the women involved were even able to climax.

That wasn't what it was like that night, though, when Anna and the two Cathys were in my bed. I had been in the living room. Anna, who was planning to sleep with me in my childhood bedroom, went in to check on the two of them, who we had given the master bedroom. When she didn't come back for a while, I went to see what was going on. I expected to find her comforting the two shell-shocked women, but instead I saw that they had pulled Anna into bed with them after she discovered them fondling and kissing one another. Anna gave me a look and nodded her head so as to ask me to join them. After I hesitantly looked into the eyes of Kathy and Catherine only to meet with a strikingly open and, for them, exceptionally vulnerable gaze, I took off my clothes and climbed in. The four of us fucked for hours. Both of the fugitives came on my cock, before I let go inside Anna as she had her third orgasm of the night with the two Cathys sucking her tits.

There was blowback from that night. Not in terms of romantic entanglement, or any jealousy having to do with our foursome. The unintended consequence of rescuing the fugitives was that the "collective" figured out just how wealthy I was. They put pressure on me to fund them, and I did. It may be unwise for me to admit to this crime, but for a brief period from late March of 1970 until early June of that year, I funded the Weatherman Underground organization as it planned for a violent revolutionary overthrow of the United States government. I cut my funding after their June 9th bombing of the New York City Police headquarters. Anna agreed with me that SDS had lost its way and, while we continued to respect their radicalism, their vision of revolution – or rather, their lack of vision – began to sharply diverge from our more mystical and utopian ideas.

In the end, all I had to do to get Rudd and Flannigan off our backs was to give them a long lecture about how Parapsychology had to be integral to the worldwide Communist revolution. I argued that its scientific approach to understanding and explaining "miracles", which had been used by theocrats in order to manipulate people, would wind up being lethal to organized religion. I sat there, in my living room, Bible-thumping my copy of *Psychic Discoveries Behind the Iron Curtain* and praising the Soviet Psychotronics program as exemplary of the Communist vision of a comprehensively scientific approach to all phenomena. Anna was amused, but tried to hide it. By the time they left, Mark and Brian looked flabbergasted and crestfallen. They wrote me off as an eccentric millionaire and one time fellow traveler.

After Anna and I distanced ourselves from the Weather Underground, I delved deeper into both existential philosophy and mystical literature under her influence. I preferred Albert Camus, Franz Kafka, and Hermann Hesse to Jean-Paul Sartre and Søren Kierkegaard. I had a love/hate relationship with Nietzsche and Dostoyevsky, one that mirrored my own inner conflict between Luciferian and Christly inclinations. How Camus had chosen to open *The Myth of Sisyphus* struck a disturbingly deep chord with me:

There is but one truly serious philosophical problem, and that is suicide. Judging whether life is or is not worth living amounts to answering the fundamental question of philosophy. All the rest — whether or not the world has three dimensions, whether the mind has nine or twelve categories — comes afterwards. These are games; one must first answer. And if it is true... that a philosopher, to deserve our respect, must preach by example, you can appreciate the importance of that reply, for it will precede the definitive act... An act like this is prepared within the silence of the heart, as is a great work of art.

Hesse's *Steppenwolf* became my favorite novel; so deeply did I identify with Harry Haller, even more profoundly than I had been able to see myself in any protagonist of Russian fiction.

For all that, I remained scientifically minded. That is not quite the right way to put it. Rather, like the narrator of Dostoyevsky's *Notes From Underground*, I saw scientific determinism as a vacuum of meaning that threatened to eviscerate my will to live in its event horizon unless an escape velocity could somehow be achieved. Whereas the certitude of mathematics once gave me solace, now the fatalism of physical laws appeared to my mind in their aspect as the unbending bars of a black iron prison of cosmic scale. The focus of my graduate work in Philosophy at the New School became deconstructing putatively 'scientific' arguments in favor of determinism — or for that matter, in defense of probabilistic randomness — with a view to reaffirming our existential freedom. I saw the empirical evidence for mind over matter that had been martialed by Parapsychology as the key to taking apart both the mechanistic determinism and sheer randomness (at a quantum level) that, taken together, characterized the predominant view of nature in modern Physics. This brought me back to Gary, who by now had a position at Rockefeller University. He enlisted me as his research assistant. I would walk from home down the East River promenade to join him there on the days that I was not at the New School.

It was mid October of 1971 when Gary called me into his office at Rockefeller University to divulge what was then a closely guarded secret. I had spent that day, and the several days before it, watching coverage of the 2,500th anniversary of the Persian Empire, which was being broadcast from Persepolis by the Shah of Iran. The Shah's speech at the tomb of Cyrus the Great during the greatest of all gatherings of the world's heads of state was hair-raising and became seared in my memory:

> Cyrus: Great King, King of Kings, King of the Achaemenids, King of this Aryan Land, from my person, King of Kings of Iran, and on behalf of my folk, hail unto you!
>
> In this splendorous moment of Iranian history, I and all Iranians, all children of this ancient Empire, that 2,500 years ago was founded by your hand, stand worshipfully before your tomb and honor your immortal memory. All of us are gathered here at this time, wherein a new Iran endowed by honorable ancient virtues establishes a fresh covenant.
>
> …We promise that the standard you raised 2,500 years ago, will remain proudly in view. We promise that the greatness and glory of this nation shall be safeguarded with an iron will, as a sacred consignment from our ancestors, and that this national heritage — more victorious than ever — will be handed down to future generations. We promise to remain true to the tradition of humanitarianism and pure contemplation that you established as the foundation of the Imperium of Iran.
>
> In these 2,500 years your country and mine, was subjected to the most burdensome catastrophes, but in all that this nation never surrendered its soul in the face of grave misfortunes… Many people showed their faces in this land with a view to upending it, but all of them left and Iran has remained in place. And during all that time, Iran endured as a beacon of the cultivation of virtue and profound contemplation.
>
> We, now, have come here to tell you, proudly: that after the passing of 25 centuries, today, like unto your honorable epoch, the flag of the Aryan Imperium flies triumphantly; that today, like unto your honorable epoch, the name of Iran is spoken around the globe with reverential praise; that today, as in your day, Iran is — in this troubled and chaotic world — a

messenger of free spiritedness and humanitarianism, and a guardian of the highest ideals of human existence. That torch which you lit, and which in these 2,500 years has never been blown out by the whirlwinds of calamity, burns more steadily and brightly than ever before in this land—and the aura of that fire, like in your time, has shone well beyond the borders of this Aryan land.

Cyrus—great king, king over all kings, the most free-spirited man amongst free men, and the champion of Iranian and world history: sleep soundly, for we are awake and shall remain vigilant!

For some reason that had not been clear to me at the time, this Fascist spectacle gave me goose bumps and made my hair stand on end. Frankly, at times, I even got heart palpitations watching it. So I remember clearly when the phone rang during the televised broadcast of the military parade at Persepolis, showcasing Persian soldiers from every epoch of Iran's long history. It was Gary, asking me to come down and see him at his office.

Our usual work at Rockefeller University consisted of developing theoretical Physics models that could accommodate parapsychological phenomena such as precognition and psychokinesis. In addition to his proposal of tachyons as a causal mechanism for these uncanny abilities, Feinberg was also developing a model of the universe with eight dimensions rather than the standard four-dimensional space-time. I was working with him on the formulation of this hyper-dimensional Physics, the equations of which were supposed to accommodate clairvoyance of future times and places. But that day he had not called me in to talk about theoretical matters.

When I arrived at his office I found that Gary's manner was even more excited than usual. The professor's eyes sparkled and there was an almost boyish mischievousness about his evident inability to keep some colossal secret that had been revealed to him by his government contacts. He had to tell me, but only after swearing me to secrecy. First he closed the door of his office, then he paced almost frantically back and forth, before deciding that he didn't feel safe discussing these matters with me there. So we went out and sat on a secluded bench near the geodesic dome on campus.

Professor Feinberg looked around nervously. Then he leaned in and whispered, "They've decided to catch up with the Russians in Psychotronics. Not just to catch up, but to beat them as badly as we have in the space race and the arms race." I gave him a penetrating, wide-eyed look. In the past year, we had often discussed what *Psychic Discoveries* had disclosed about Psi research in the USSR and its Eastern bloc satellite states. "This is no joke, Nick, they're going to do it." I asked, "Who, exactly?" His eyes darted around again in a paranoiac fashion. "It's being funded by the CIA, but the pilot research and development will be done at the Stanford Research Institute in Palo Alto. Two physicists with security clearances are running the program. That's how I heard about it. They called me to help them figure out what to tell the Senators when they ask *how* this weird stuff *works*, you know, theoretically. They need to tell some kind of story convincing enough to laymen so that the Senate Intelligence committee rubber stamps the classified budget for the program. They're calling it 'remote viewing' to make it sound more technical."

I sat back, sinking into the bench and into a staggering train of thought. Gary was leaning forward with his elbows on his knees. When I next opened my mouth, still struggling to decide which of the many questions racing through my mind to ask first, he cocked his neck to look at me. "And they're going to use this for *what*?" Gary had a positively devilish look on his face. "Everything," he said. "Operationally?!" He nodded affirmatively in reply. "There's a psychic here in New York who is already working with them to develop the protocol. He's an artist. Ingo Swann. I want you to come with me to see him before he leaves for Palo Alto, where he's going to be living for a while to help Puthoff and Targ develop the program. They're the physicists. Hal Puthoff, who I know from other classified work that we've done together, and some guy called Russell Targ. The CIA has its doubts about whether Targ has the stomach for everything they plan to do with these 'abilities' once they've rendered them reliable." I took a long, deep breath. The most dangerous and deadly chapter of my life was about to begin. I got the sense that everything else had been preparation.

CHAPTER 3

ARYAN APOCALYPSE

Gary and I went to see Swann, the psychic artist, who was living at an apartment in the Bowery. He was a flaming faggot, not that I minded much. What bothered me more than his annoying mannerisms was that a cursory look through his bookshelf made it clear that Ingo was a member of the Church of Scientology. Parts of his relatively small library looked like the L. Ron Hubbard required reading list. His paintings were technically impressive, but had the same lurid and garish quality characteristic of *Battlefield Earth* and Hubbard's even lesser works. I looked over at Gary silently, with an expression that he had no trouble interpreting as some cross between dismay and contemptuous skepticism. Feinberg looked back in such a manner as to reassure me and urge me to be patient. The professor turned out to be right.

Ingo Swann's abilities as a psychic were truly remarkable. He picked up on my cynical attitude and was so affronted by it that he reached right into my mind, or as he might put it, reached out into past places and times, to confront me with information about my life that he could hardly have known. Some of this concerned my aunt, and I had to stop Ingo before he embarrassed me in front of Gary who was starting to look very uncomfortable. He had the decency never to ask me to elaborate on what Swann was getting at that day when I cut him off.

What Professor Feinberg did ask me about was the following exchange. Late into our visit to his apartment, the artist leaned back into his armchair and looked arrogantly at me while Gary and I sat across from him on the sofa. He stopped sipping his coffee, and blurted out, "He doesn't know, does he? You never told him – about your abilities." I gave him a curt look and a nod that wordlessly said, "shut up." Ingo hissed while smirking. He knew that I would never disrespect him again. As for Gary, I had to explain to him that my interest in psychic phenomena was not purely intellectual, and that I had experienced more than the odd incident or two of telepathy or precognition that I confessed to when he shared similar trivialities with me as if they were unspeakably marvelous. Given the project at SRI that Gary was unofficially reading me into, the time was right for this confession. I admitted to a lifetime of intense psychic experiences, uncanny abilities that were strongest in my childhood but that had persisted in some measure all the way to the present. Ingo could see it — I don't know, in my 'aura' or something. I guess it takes one to know one. Later he would tell Puthoff and Targ at SRI that when we first met it was like an incandescent light bulb of psychic energy had walked into his studio.

By the time I finished my master's degree at the New School in May of 1972, I had been extended an invitation to join Ingo at SRI to undergo the "remote viewing" training protocol. Officially, the invitation came from Gary's colleague, Hal Puthoff. Or rather, I should say that "unofficially" and on the face of it, Hal invited me. However, I knew full well that being invited to participate in such a project meant that I had already undergone a thorough background check and received security clearance by the CIA. When I thought back to the intense interest I had in Communism during my teenage years, and then *my involvement with the Weathermen* only a couple of years earlier, I found this whole situation to be astonishingly ironic. It was hard to imagine that they hadn't dug these things up, especially considering the fact that they were working with psychics — including a certain Pat Price, who had done clairvoyant work for Police departments. But then it occurred to me: *they were working with psychics.* Clairvoyants and other occult adepts are notoriously eccentric and volatile people. My shady past was par for the course. Apparently, they had also grasped the connection between especially strong psychic ability and a history of trauma. So what I suffered in childhood was also of interest to them. It was seen as a qualification, not to say, an initiation that cracked my mind open to exceptional perceptions.

Anna did not want me to travel to California, even if the training program was supposed to take only six months — or less, if I proved to have the aptitude that they were anticipating. It wasn't as if I was giving up my apartment, and I insisted that she make it her own home while I was away. She had been hoping that I would go straight into doctoral studies at the New School, where she had just entered the Philosophy department to pursue her MA after having graduated from Barnard. We fought about it, and then she felt ashamed for trying to hold me back from fulfilling my potential. Anna was full of trepidation, but she feigned a stiff upper lip and let me go. When I was about to part with her at the airport to get onto my Pan-Am flight to San Francisco, she almost fell apart. It was painful to see.

That first night in California I stayed at a hotel in San Francisco with a spectacular view of the Transamerica Pyramid amidst the downtown skyline. A driver in a black limousine picked me up in the morning and drove me down to Palo Alto, where I met Harold Puthoff in person for the first time. He introduced me to his associate, Russell Targ. Ingo was also there, and despite his typical freshness, he seemed genuinely delighted to see me (maybe he thought, or hoped, that I was a closeted homosexual). My first "target" turned out to be another building on the Stanford University campus. Of course, I did not know that until after the session was over.

It was chosen because of the distinctive pattern carved into its stucco walls. These consisted of repeating squares that were made up of four rectangular cutouts in the orientation of a Swastika, with another smaller square in the middle of the four 'arms.' There were also trees and dense shrubbery beneath the walkway that stretched around the rectilinear atrium inside the building, and this was supposed to give me a material that would starkly contrast with the stucco and concrete, both in texture and color. Beginning with the Swastika pattern, which I sketched out right away, I either visually depicted or verbally described all of these features in a degree of detail that stunned Dr. Puthoff and even made Ingo envious. There were also lamps hanging down from the tall ceilings which my sketch and notes portrayed as "something like flying saucers... metallic, copper." I even picked up on these spherical bands of intersecting metal that reminded me of "gyroscopes." They turned out to be another kind of lights, or rather an open mesh casing for single light bulbs, suspended from the ceiling of a hallway on the second floor whose windows without glass looked out onto the aforementioned atrium.

Finally, Russell Targ took me to see the building, squinting at it all the while through the thick glasses that only moderately improved his poor eyesight. It was the "Oakes Laboratories of Radiology and Biophysics." That I was allowed to tour the site meant that Targ and Puthoff were opening up the possibility that the information in my "remote viewing" session was actually obtained through precognition (whatever that means). I may have described *what I was going to see.* In any case, the confirmation was literally breathtaking. It really boosted my confidence, and so I learned *fast.*

The core of the training was to learn how to separate your interpretation of an unknown "target" placed inside of an envelope from the elemental impressions of it that you received through Extrasensory Perception (ESP). This was like learning disciplined meditation, quieting the mind's analytical faculties so that analysis could be left to the intelligence agents who would receive the "data" from any given session. One was never supposed to come into contact with these analysts, since they had knowledge of the target, or would have such knowledge, when doing their analysis. Impressions received were recorded both visually and verbally. An almost hieroglyphic visual language had been developed for quickly indicating the presence of flowing water, trees, or manmade structures in a few quick strokes without the mind interfering with interpretive overlay as one struggled to draw one's indistinct impressions. But this was designed for future recruits who were not expected to have any artistic ability. Although I was not as skilled as Ingo, I actually had considerable artistic talent despite my focus on mathematics and science. I excelled at drawing in High School, and my aunt had often offered herself as a nude model to encourage me to develop my talent. So I quickly dispensed with SRI's symbolic system.

There was also a checklist that had to be filled, which broke up and classified impressions in terms of a long series of predefined characteristics. This was meant to help determine whether a site was artificial or manmade, whether it was indoors or outdoors, whether there was water, if it was light or dark, or alternating at various times. These are only a few examples, the list was very long and by analyzing the checkmarks that were supposed to be made without conscious reflection, an analyst would be able to form a composite image of the site. The aim here was to be able to 'look inside' clandestine Soviet facilities that were, say, masked by a seemingly natural landscape, like a weapons manufacturing facility deep inside a large hillside. If the checklist showed "artificial", "concrete", "electricity", etc. where there was only supposed to be a hill, that would tend to confirm other intelligence that indicated to the CIA that the Soviets had a secret facility at this locale.

When trying to focus on such a site, sometimes one would receive impressions of that place at a time in the past *or in the future*. It became clear that the mind would often be magnetically drawn to the target site at that time when it was giving off the most psychic energy, in effect, when the most intensely interesting things were going on there. At first this was a distraction from gathering intelligence in real time, but it did not take long for the CIA to recognize the tremendous value of such a capability. Soon Ingo Swann, Pat Price, and I were being trained to move backwards and forwards in time as well as clairvoyantly view places remote in space.

I learned all this and more, but becoming a master of any art or craft means letting go of studied discipline and allowing it to become fully internalized skill that effortlessly channels what had been raw talent. That was just as true in the case of "remote viewing." After a couple of months of intensive training, I was allowed to let go of the guardrails. In fact, Hal Puthoff encouraged me to do so. We conducted these relatively unstructured sessions privately — well, even more privately than the rest of the program. He instructed me not to inform Targ of what we were doing together. It turned out that both Pat Price and Ingo Swann were also doing sessions like this "off the record." I would do mine back at the furnished rental apartment on the Stanford campus that had been cleared for the duration of my stay.

The target for these sessions was 'chosen' by me, albeit unconsciously. It was not long after I began recording the impressions that I realized what had come together from out of my subconscious in order to select the target. For some reason, which was about to become clear to me, the recurring nightmares of nuclear war that I was afflicted with during my late teens interlocked with the terrible foreboding, even panic, that I felt while watching media coverage of the 2,500th anniversary of the Persian Empire that day that Gary called and had me come down to Rockefeller University, where he read me into *this* SRI program that I was in right now.

Three flashes of light in the desert, and the Shah of Iran's proudly determined face – as if he had seized lightning within his grasp, like Zeus or Indra. That was the first image that I got. With my history of morbid fascination with nuclear war, it hardly required much "analytical overlay" to conclude that I was watching Iran's first atomic bomb test. Later, the details of the terrain that I noted even allowed me to identify which desert this was. The Persians have two vast deserts sweeping across the East of Iran. This was the Lot Desert, rather ominously named after the prophet from the story of Sodom's destruction. It took countless hours, over many days, to nail down the date – at least to the year. I did that in part by focusing on one of the other individuals whose image kept prominently appearing in these sessions. Our President, Richard Nixon. Despite deep concerns and some harsh criticisms of the Shah being voiced by international media, Nixon had put in a private phone call to congratulate his friend on bringing Iran into the club of nuclear armed nations. I saw this phone call, and heard Nixon assuring Pahlavi that the bad press would blow over. I also telepathically picked up on the fact that, despite his reassurances to the Shah, in the back of his mind Nixon was concerned that his refusal to punish Iran for violating the Nuclear Non-Proliferation Treaty (NPT) would become a campaign issue over the coming year, especially against a rival like Jimmy Carter, who was so critical of Pahlavi's human rights record. So Iran's successful nuclear weapons test would take place sometime around the fall of 1975.

The King of Kings would not bask in the glory of those lightning bolts for long. I saw his country shaken, and then shattered, by a violent Communist revolution. Nixon was now in his third term as President. I saw him offering the Shah his full support, morally and materially, to confront the mass of demonstrators and the cadres of armed insurgents with brutal force. The Imperial Iranian military was deployed in the streets of Tehran and other Persian cities. It seemed, our President had his own share of similar troubles at home, which made him more than empathetic to Pahlavi. America appeared to me to have become a police state.

The Shah believed, with good reason, that the leftist protesters and guerrilla fighters rebelling against his rule represented an orchestrated attempt by the Soviet Union to seize Iran, together with the warm water ports and vast petroleum resources of the Persian Gulf. Such an economic boon would almost certainly secure a Russian victory in the Cold War. I write "with good reason" because the Shah had, some months prior to the uprising in Iran, witnessed a Soviet invasion of Afghanistan – a country whose northern half still spoke Persian, and which was an artificial state carved out of Eastern Iran by British colonialists in the mid-19th century. In Afghanistan a leftwing revolution, which was hardly organic, had established a Communist regime. When this nascent Soviet Republic was threatened by radical Islamic insurgents and feudal landlords, its Prime Minister, a man whose name I could discern as Amin, invited "assistance" from the Russians, who sent troops across the border. By the time the Communist uprising against the Shah began, Soviet troops were occupying Afghanistan and the USSR had lengthened its already long border with Iran.

Mohammad Reza Pahlavi had been traumatized in his youth by helplessly watching as his father, Reza Shah "the Great", was forcibly exiled from Iran in 1941 by both Allied *and Soviet occupying troops.* While British and American forces agreed to leave at the conclusion of the Second World War, the Russians tried to stay. They stoked secessionist insurgencies in several parts of northern Iran and, for a brief time, succeeded in setting up Soviet Socialist Republics in occupied Iranian Kurdistan and Azerbaijan – amalgamating the latter to the northern part of Azerbaijan that the Russian Empire had already seized from Iran in the Russo-Persian Wars of the 1800s. These 19th century wars were a disaster wherein the Persians lost about a third of their territory, some of the "stans" of Central Asia (*ostan* means "province" in Persian), to the Russian Czar. The Shah had repeatedly gone on record, in interviews with the international media, that he would sooner see Iran destroyed than humiliatingly occupied once more by foreign forces. He had warned, "If you think you can come here again, you should know that there will only be ruins for you to occupy."

Moreover, anyone with half a brain, let alone someone as intelligent as Pahlavi, could see that the Russians had no intrinsic interest whatsoever in a godforsaken country like Afghanistan. What they had done there was a dry run and staging ground for the planned Soviet invasion of Iran. The CIA concurred with this analysis and Langley was already coordinating with SAVAK to turn Iran into the bastion of resistance against Soviet expansion into the Islamic world. The Shah was tasked with funneling funding and arms to the *Mojaheddin* led by Ahmad Shah Masoud, in Persian-speaking northern Afghanistan. As best as I could piece it together from my precognitive clairvoyance and telepathic penetration of the intentions of the various players involved, what happened next would be worthy of the annals of martial hubris. You see, few people knew that the Shah was dying of cancer and that he did not have years to sustain a drawn-out resistance against the Russians in Afghanistan, especially now that his own regime was in danger of being overthrown by Soviet-backed leftists. Believing that his friend Richard Nixon, however upset, would still back him after the fact, the Shah ordered the Imperial Iranian Air Force to attack Soviet positions in Afghanistan.

From what I could tell, it was the summer of 1980, because a lot of psychic energy was focused on the fact that many countries, including America, had to boycott the Olympic Games being held in Moscow in order to demonstrate their disapproval of the Soviet aggression in Afghanistan. There was also dismay over the fact that the 1984 Winter Olympic Games were scheduled to be held in Iran, where the Shah had invested in building massive ski resorts and other winter sports facilities. People were concerned about whether another round of the Olympics would be ruined by unrest. That ought to have been the least of their concerns.

The Iranian airstrikes against Russian positions in Afghanistan were devastating. Within 48 hours, the Shah had pulverized Soviet forces, especially those positioned closest to the Afghan border with Iran. At the close of this operation, he carried out his second nuclear weapons test, this time in the Kavir Desert, close enough to the Afghan border for the atomic flash to be seen by Soviet troops. He intended it as a warning flare. Then, he declared the protesters and insurgents on the streets of Iran's cities to be the fifth column of a foreign enemy, namely the Soviet Union. Imperial Iranian Air Force helicopters were ordered to strafe strongholds of guerrilla fighters, and even large gatherings of unarmed protesters who refused to disperse. Never has there been a grander and more costly strategic miscalculation. After taking a few days to absorb the initial shock of the Shah's preemptive strike, the politburo in Moscow ordered the Red Army to mass along the entire Soviet border with Iran, all the way from Azerbaijan in the Caucasus, around the Caspian Sea, through Turkmenistan and down into the new Afghan extension of this border. Under the pretext of protecting "the People's Soviet Revolution" in Iran from a "brutal American-backed dictator", the Soviet Union invaded Iran. Numbers, including specific dates, are very hard to nail down in remote viewing, but I was able to narrow the timeframe to mid-July of 1980, in part because the Olympic games in Moscow were prematurely suspended by a declared state of emergency.

The Shah engaged the Soviet troops with his own massive army, his often criticized purchase of hundreds of tanks now having been more than justified by the turn of events. Pahlavi waited for foreign civilians attending the Olympics to be cleared out of Moscow by emergency flights, before the Russians closed their airports in the capital as they had elsewhere in the USSR. Then, sometime in August of 1980, Soviet troops who had already occupied Tabriz finally converged on Tehran and entered the Persian capital from three directions — the west, coming from already occupied Iranian Kurdistan, the northwest, from occupied Azerbaijan, and the east, from occupied Khorasan.

Shâhanshâh Âryâmehr, the "King of Kings, and Light of the Aryans", gave his final command from a bunker deep inside the Alborz mountains. Three heavy payload long-range bombers were prepared for a kamikaze strike, which it was hoped that at least one of them would succeed in carrying out. Each was carrying an atomic bomb spray-painted with Persian calligraphy that read, "Never Again. Death to Russia! Long live Iran! Long live the Emperor!" (*Dobâreh hargez. Marg bar Roussiye! Pâyandeh Irân! Jâvid Shâh!*) To my horror,

I watched with my mind's eye as one of them did get through Soviet air defenses to deliver its payload.

Moscow was obliterated. It all happened so fast that most of a ruined world would never be able to piece together who struck first or why. Within minutes of the attack on Moscow, the Soviet high command declared martial law and determined that the Shah of Iran had acted as a proxy of his close ally, the United States. Before Pahlavi could even broadcast his planned emergency address announcing his nuclear response to the Russian invasion of Iran, he and his staff watched from their bunker as every television station in the United States went dark. The Soviet Union had let loose their rain of ICBMs in what they considered a retaliatory strike on America, one so severe that its intention was to prevent a counterstrike. But Nixon, who was warned by NORAD of the incoming missiles, did manage to get America's own arsenal out of the silos so as to rain fire down on Russia. The Light of the Aryans had brought our world to a fiery end, one worthy of the ancient Zoroastrian prophecies of a global firestorm at the Apocalypse.

Hal Puthoff was almost as appalled by what came out of these sessions as I was. Anna was unnerved that I could not tell her over the phone why it was that I sounded so exhausted and on edge, why I wasn't getting more than a few hours of erratic sleep each night. The nightmares from my teenage years had come back, but now, instead of just being a vision of the thermonuclear incineration of New York, they were filled in with the details of this Aryan Apocalypse unleashed by the self-styled King of Kings.

One sleepless night, Hal came by exceptionally late and asked me to pour us a couple of drinks. (I had a minibar.) He sat in an armchair across from me as I leaned back into the sofa with my drink, eager to hear something that he was obviously itching to say. It turned out that the "data" from my freeform sessions on the Soviet invasion of Iran had struck a nerve somewhere high up in the CIA. I said, cynically, "Let me guess, the CIA wants to hire me fulltime?" He shook his head.

Hal had a guarded manner of speaking but, by the way he was bending his neck down and looking up at me, I could tell that he wanted to share something with me, but was only allowed to tell me as much as I "need to know."

After reiterating the extreme confidentiality of this conversation, he confessed that another psychic espionage unit was being set up. It wasn't only going to be involved in "remote viewing" but also in "remote influencing." It would even attempt *to change a pre-cognized future*. Targ would never be read into this other operation, which was not being run by the CIA but by Naval Intelligence. He could see me struggling to understand why the Navy would be developing a program parallel to the one being set up by the CIA, and even penetrating the CIA program in order to mine it for data and, as I was about to discover, harvest it for the top talent.

Hal asked me, "Nick, has it ever occurred to you that 70% of this planet's surface is covered by the oceans?" Then he continued, "Well, Naval Intelligence wants to know *what is going on down there*." I stared at him somewhat incredulously, as if to say, "Going on *under* the oceans?", while I wondered why the hell Naval Intelligence officers would be interested in the marine biology of squids and sperm whales. Then, as if tiring of the charade, he blurted out, "More than fifty percent of UFOs are seen entering or exiting the Earth's oceans." I almost dropped my drink when I tried to set it down on the table. A chill ran through my body, all the way up my spine, making the back of my neck break out into a cold sweat. I tried to suppress a shudder, but Hal saw it.

After an awkward silence, I looked dead into his eyes and said, "I understand, Sir." It was the first time that I called Dr. Puthoff, "Sir." It was also the first time I realized who *or what* I was dealing with. "I knew you would," he said, and nodded his head. "We want *you* — for the *other* unit." From the shit-eating grin on his face he seemed to relish that he knew what my next question was going to be. "Where's it going to be based?" I asked. "New York City," he said, with a diabolical smile. "We've acquired a floor in the North Tower of the new World Trade Center. Well, technically, it belongs to the NSA, but we're leasing it from them."

I did not recognize the acronym. "NSA??? You mean NASA?" He was annoyed with himself at having said somewhat more than he was supposed to say, and then, after taking a gulp of Scotch, grumbled almost under his breath, "National Security Agency. You've never heard of it because as far as the public is concerned, it doesn't exist." It was interesting that he said "we're" when he shared that Naval Intelligence was leasing one of the floors that this "National Security Agency" had apparently bought in the Twin Towers, the construction of which was just barely being completed at the time. So, Puthoff was Naval Intelligence. "Interesting," I thought to myself.

"One last thing, Nikolai. When you get back to New York and start working at the facility, don't mention any of this to Gary. I know you'll be tempted. But he doesn't have clearance." That really awed me. I know that intelligence is compartmentalized, but I couldn't believe that, with all Feinberg's government and think tank connections, which informed his writing of *The Prometheus Project*, I was being let in on something that he had no "need to know." How was I supposed to explain to him that I was not going to go straight into a PhD program? What was I supposed to tell Anna?! I suppose Hal didn't mention her, not because she evaded the CIA's background check, but because he knew all too well that I could never lie to her. Of course, that also meant that she would become a liability for them.

Anna was ecstatic to hear that I was heading home early, especially since it was almost Christmas. She had tried to sound strong over the phone when we would talk at night, but I could tell that she was straining to steel herself against nearly uncontrollable emotions having to do with issues of abandonment and separation anxiety that had roots in her childhood, which was almost as troubled as mine. She surprised me by showing up to La Guardia airport when my flight arrived. I suddenly saw her running toward me at the gate in the black fur coat that I had gotten her, and the next thing I knew she had thrown her arms around me and was practically weeping as she tightened her grip. I kissed the tears off her face.

When we got back to my apartment I saw that, as soon as she heard I was coming home ahead of schedule, she had gone out and gotten a Christmas tree. She had already strung the lights on it, and was waiting to do the rest of the decorations together. Some of my ornaments were ornately painted Russian Orthodox eggs, with icons framed by sparkling gold and silver patterns. I remember that night as one of the happiest in my life. Maybe the happiest of all. I could hardly have imagined that I was about to look into the cold, dark depths of hell.

CHAPTER 4

ATLANTIS RESURFACING

℧ he views over New York City from the Naval Intelligence offices hidden on the 79th floor of the World Trade Center's North Tower were breathtakingly spectacular. Unfortunately, remote viewers such as myself had to do their sessions in a window-less room that was uniformly painted battleship grey. The reduction of sensory stimuli was part of the protocol for enhancing the data that we obtained through clairvoyance and precognition. When I walked off the elevator on the first morning at my new job, I had hardly cleared the false façade of the front hallway where I was given my badge by the secretary, when I heard someone shout "So, you're the philosopher!" An overly self-confident, not to say arrogant, man wearing a loosened necktie, and a blue-grey suit that was a little too tight for him, got up from his desk and came over to shake my hand. Somewhat defensively, I replied, "I also have a degree in Physics." Jack nodded jovially as he patted my shoulder. "That's one of the reasons Hal sent you. He's a good friend of mine." Jack was to be my handler and guide for our work in the grey room.

By the end of the first day on the job, my life would never be the same. Granted, it felt as if I was only half remembering things that I had once known but was made to forget. Still, breaking the locks on that part of my mind meant opening a floodgate that would eventually lead to my drowning. Within the first two hours of our remote viewing sessions together, Jack had me describing UFOs to him as they dove into the Atlantic Ocean off the coast of Antarctica. Some of these craft were polished and shining silvery discs, others were more dull-grey wingless cigar-shaped vehicles with windows that glowed blue at night.

When I was tasked with looking into these windows, and following the occupants of the UFOs down into the dark ocean depths, I experienced something that my training had not prepared me for. I was blocked. They knew that I was spying on them, and they tried their best to block me. I reported this to Jack. He nodded wearily but gave me a glance of appreciation as well, as if to signal both that they had been having this problem for a long time and also that I was clearly on target. I persisted and, by the end of my first week of sessions, I was delivering clearer data about the targets than anyone who had worked them before me.

At that point, I was fully briefed by Jack regarding the intelligence already gathered through this project. This information was not limited to the vast submarine city built into the continental shelf of Antarctica, or the one beneath Lake Vostok. In addition to these sites, the remote viewers here at Naval Intelligence had discovered extensive structures on the dark side of the Moon and on Mars. I say "structures" because these far exceeded the scale and complexity of bases. They were the size of cities, and some of them were vastly ancient. Clairvoyantly following some of the saucer and cigar-shaped craft lifting off from Antarctica had led my fellow psychic spies to these other locations.

On the dark side of the Moon there was at least one large city, the remote viewing of which had been confirmed by feedback in the form of classified National Reconnaissance Office satellites positioned in the lunar orbit. Jack laid the photographs out in front of me. There were various polygonal structures, and some spherical ones as well, with one monolithic tower or obelisk of staggering height. All of these buildings were titanic in scale, and appeared to be built (or carved?) out of something like stone (perhaps it was concrete). In any case, they were not metallic. There were also photographs of tread marks from tractors that appeared to be involved in mining operations.

By far the most disturbing discovery on the Moon was that these structures on the lunar surface were like the tip of an iceberg that extended deep beneath the moon dust, down into *a vast artificial structure!* As described by those on the project before my arrival, the Moon was largely hollow and its interior surface was honeycombed with constructions of dazzling complexity and varying antiquity. The remote viewers who had been tasked with describing the cavernous lunar interior all had the impression that the Moon was actually older than the Earth and that it had been parked in Earth's orbit. Moreover, those who had piloted this cloaked space station were responsible for some gargantuan geo-engineering project on the Earth, a sort of remaking of the ecological and biological matrix of the planet in such a manner as would be conducive to the guided evolution of humanoid life in place of the dinosaurs then dominant here. These engineers appeared to be from Mars, and their urgency to reshape the Earth had to do with some horrifically unnatural catastrophe that they had suffered there attendant to the deliberate and total destruction of a gigantic Earth-like home world that had been located between Mars and Jupiter. The asteroid belt that is there today consists of its remaining fragments.

Jack explained that there was, as yet, no feedback for what was remotely viewed on Mars. However, the psychically gathered data had been sent up the chain of command and had succeeded in convincing those who represented the National Security establishment within NASA to target this region of Mars, namely Cydonia, as a focus of photography that would be sent back from the Viking probe within a year or two. The problem would then be to prevent this photographic confirmation, should it be forthcoming, from entering the public domain. "If the masses — of any society on Earth — were to learn of what we had already psychically spied on the surface of Cydonia, let alone beneath the surface of Mars," Jack explained as I nodded gravely, "the psychological, economic, and political consequences would be catastrophic."

Jack showed me the sketches and notes from remote viewing sessions regarding Mars. By far the most impressive structure was a pentagonal pyramid that seemed to be several times larger than the Great Pyramid of Giza. Not far from it was a sort of Sphinx. Well, a sphinx like head at any rate, whose face was carved out of a huge rocky outcrop so that it stared up at the remote viewers looking down at the surface. Sphinx like because it appeared to have a headdress. There was something vaguely 'Egyptian' about it. Although it was badly eroded, blasted and almost pulverized, a hauntingly foreboding expression of regret seemed etched into the face, together with a single teardrop.

There was one place, within a crater, where a geometrically regular checkerboard type pattern could be seen, which was suspected to be the remnant of ruined buildings. These were vastly ancient, primordial. By contrast, there was a newer metallic structure — a tall antenna type device that was bent. Those who focused on this structure were led, by association, down some air vents into a labyrinthine maze of subterranean tunnels that showed signs of having been damaged by explosions. Only a few of these were still intact, and they provided access to a city deep beneath the surface of Cydonia. Attempts to view the goings-on in this city were, however, repeatedly blocked by those who lived and worked there, and who apparently have psychic powers that dwarf our own.

I'll never forget how my heart sank the first time that I managed to follow these people piloting their craft into one of their lairs back here on Earth. Yes, they were *people* – more or less like us. They were as tall as professional basketball players and had the build of Olympic swimmers. Their faces looked like those of Nordic supermodels, except with more chiseled features and sunken eye sockets that made their almond-shaped brilliant blue or green eyes look preternaturally large. Their skulls were slightly tapered and a little taller than the cranium of your average Scandinavian, but in the men and women alike this was largely concealed by shoulder-length hair. This platinum blond, red, or jet black hair was straight and very thick, combining qualities that we associate with Caucasian, Asian, and Semitic hair. The men were beardless and longhaired, so that the main feature distinguishing the women from the men were the full breasts of the former. All were wearing skintight uniforms of a pale greyish-blue color.

They disembarked from their craft in long tubular docks cut into the rock of the continental shelf. There was something mesmeric about the way they walked. No small talk or jesting or gestures expressing individual personality. They hardly even looked at each other, and yet it was as if they were moved by a single mind — or a single-mindedness inconceivable to us. A group of greyish humanoids that were very short (by comparison) trailed along behind them. Their heads kind of looked like those of overgrown fetuses, bald with huge black almond-shaped eyes, a vestigial nose, over a slit for a mouth, beneath which was a pointy chin. Their bodies were slim and sleek and almost seemed to float off the ground. They had very long, thin arms ending in four slender digits. When briefing me on Antarctica, the Moon, and Mars, Jack had informed me that these things were biomechanical robots, which were manufactured to carry out various complex tasks and to function in high risk situations, such as handling abductees.

I followed the Nordic types into their abode, and this is where what I saw made me succumb to a terrible sinking feeling that I was never really able to shake. The place was carved out of solid rock, in some places very smoothly, such as the polished floor, whereas in others the jagged walls had been left in a more natural state. It was very dark, lit only by the eerie greenish glow of phosphorescent stones of spherical and rectangular shapes that had been set into the walls and in certain places along the floor, especially the sides of stairways. These stairways had very broad steps that fit together with the titanic scale of everything else in this place, including high ceilings that contributed to an atmosphere of cathedral gloom. Along some of the walkways, including the very first one that I saw, were immense floor to ceiling windows. Seeing the ocean like that, with a jagged rock wall on the other side of me, was almost heart-stopping. My blood ran cold from fright, especially when I was able to make out the contours of a sperm whale with a giant squid locked into its jaws, not far from the glass. It reminded me of a diorama at the Museum of Natural History, but these were *alive*. In fact, I could feel their vital force behind the windows before I was able to see them.

After this experience, I went back to the museum to see this diorama. It was one of the dioramas on the bottom floor of the gigantic atrium that was the Millstein Hall for Ocean Life, with a grey whale suspended from its ceiling. What I did that night at the Museum of Natural History was a reflection of the state of mind that I found myself in after only a couple of weeks of remote viewing these submarine targets for Naval Intelligence. Near closing time, I found a restroom in an obscure wing of the museum, one that showcased small tribal artifacts that were part of ritual Shamanism. With my feet up on the lid of a toilet, inside a locked stall, I hid until my watch read that it was a full two hours after the building had been cleared out. In those days, there were no motion sensors to sound an alarm. Just a few night guards spread far between, mainly at the entrances and exits.

I wound my way through the wooden hallways full of gigantically more-than-life sized models of earth-boring worms and other insects, until I was back at the Hall of Ocean Life. It was even darker than usual, but that is what I wanted. I was seeking a Shamanic experience of sorts, an initiatory ordeal that would help me to overcome the terror that I felt in those occulted places that I had been remote viewing, so that I could more perspicaciously perceive what their denizens were doing. It upset me that Anna would be worried sick when I did not come home. Overcoming that binding tie to this life and this world was, however, to my mind part of the ordeal. Little did I know that I would find her again on another level altogether that night in the dark heart of the museum's oceanic simulacrum.

I slowly descended the steps, and then laid down under the whale with my initial trial being to overcome the uneasy feeling that it might fall on me. After hours of meditatively following flashbacks of what I had seen from that grey room atop the Twin Towers, and gleaning a few more glimpses into those underwater lairs, I either fell asleep or entered an altered state of consciousness that made the museum disappear into the ambient darkness. How long I remained in that state I do not know, but I awakened from out of it quite suddenly – not into the Hall of Ocean Life, but into a nightmare so terrible that many of us have chosen to collectively forget it.

The stars were brighter than I had ever seen in this life, especially in the sky over a city, and they were falling. It was as if the heavens had been unhinged. There, suspended high above us against the writhing Milky Way, was a ghostly white sperm whale tossed out of the depths by the tsunami whose mile-high tidal wave was closing in on us fast. We could feel the ocean spray in our faces. Despite her changed features I recognized Anna at once. We were holding hands, tightening our grip as we braced ourselves to sink together with this world lost in a storm of dark wisdom.

After I snuck out of the museum the next morning and finally made it home to her, before she could rebuke me for going missing I burst out weeping in her arms. Frankly, I can't even clearly remember how I got home. New York seemed utterly alien to me. What I *do* remember, and what I lamentably shared with her, was the flood of memories that pounded the battlements of my soul that night on the floor of the Hall of Ocean Life.

The city that I saw destroyed by the tsunami, and by whatever ungodly upheaval of the earth made the stars appear to fall, was like no city in recorded history. It was a vast metropolis, of a scale to rival

Manhattan, but built in precisely-cut megalithic stone instead of steel and concrete. Rather than skyscrapers, there were multi-tiered pyramidal and polygonal structures with colossal stairways leading up them from the broad streets. Some of the buildings were interlinked by elevated walkways with colonnades in certain places. The stars could be seen so clearly at night because there was no electric lighting.

There was certainly electricity. In fact, the sky was full of it. A hexagonal stone tower that tapered toward the top, where it terminated in a bulbous dome overhanging the structure's edges, was shooting fearsome bolts of artificial lightning into the night's sky in every direction. It also produced something like the aurora borealis, which looked spectacularly ethereal as it radiated over the city. This system was used to wirelessly broadcast electric power to machines and vehicles of various kinds, including wingless cigar-shaped airships streaking through the sky, but it was *not* used to illuminate light bulbs.

Instead of electric lighting, phosphorescent stone spheres on pillars lit the major squares, and much smaller ones set into the curbside illuminated the path ahead on those avenues that were more peripheral. The quality of this lighting made the city's denizens look creepy by sucking the color out of them and whatever they were wearing, in exactly the same way as I had seen in the submarine facilities. In fact, these were *the same* Nordic-looking people. Their clothes were different, though. Instead of the skintight uniforms, they were wearing flowing robes or coats long enough to reach their ankles, with a kind of hieroglyphics or hieratic writing running along the edge of them from where they closed around the neck all the way down to the hem.

These were not the only people in the city, and the others looked nothing like them. There were armor-clad and helmet-wearing guards whose features were similar to the Nubians of today, except that they were so black that their skin had a blue corn chip hue when it was in the sunshine. My impression was that these were policemen, or were being used as such. The whole place felt as if it was under martial law, and one was not supposed to be on the streets past certain hours without traveling papers. Then there were slaves of various kinds. Some of these hardly looked human. Perhaps they were Neanderthals or some other kind of primitive hominid. Their hair had been shaved and their hulking naked bodies were covered in a greyish paste of chalk mixed with sweat from working at the stone quarries where they would be led in chain gangs. Then there were domestic slaves who, frankly, looked most like people do now. They were not as tall as the Nordic types that they served, nor were they as ethereal. But their skulls were shaped more normally, basically indistinguishable from those of a Mediterranean or Semitic type today. They were dark haired and had brown or black eyes. Most of them were clothed simply, but there were exceptions. Certain women in particular were more exotically and extravagantly dressed than their masters, albeit also much more scantily clad, and ensconced in jewelry. They had the bodies and gait of dancers. As I knew all too well, these were courtesans.

That is putting it politely. To be honest, they were sex slaves. A great controversy surrounded their function in our society. Certain hardcore traditionalists believed that the use of these "things" — as the slaves in general were called — would corrupt us. Others contended that, since they were not conscious and did not really have souls, the sex slaves could be used just the same way as the other "things" were. They simply needed to be made more refined and skilled to carry out their tasks, which also included a variety of other work as domestic servants. A very small circle of us knew that both of these views were wrong. We had secretly committed the sin of falling in love with one or another of these women, who we found to actually be possessed of their own inner world and a character-building horizon of experience different from that of their masters. We had even removed the birth control mechanism so as to be able to interbreed with them, with a view to hybridizing their population and thereby strengthening it for a future rebellion.

The woman that I saw in the first image that came to me, the one that I was holding hands with under the falling stars and that I had

recognized as a previous incarnation of Anna, was one of these courtesans. She looked much the same as in this life, with sharp features
that were a cross between Eurasian and Mediterranean, with dark
brown hair and amber eyes. She was just as thin and graceful, with
small pointy breasts. Her bangle-studded ankles were strikingly beautiful, and so were her hands, which from fingertip to wrist, bespoke a
wisdom much older than her years and that it should not have been
possible for one of her "kind" to have attained. These "things" were
not supposed to have names, but I had given her one: *Marjâna*.

Each time she would come to me, I could tell that she was distressed from the anxiety of having passed through the several sets of
guarded cyclopean walls and presenting her papers to the sentries.
There was nothing inherently unlawful about her coming here, but
our being in love was certainly forbidden and she was afraid that
those two-legged guard dogs would almost smell it on her. Or, more
likely, that it would be noticed by another citizen. You see, this was a
telepathic society. Our thoughts were supposed to be open to one another. It is almost impossible to explain to a modern man what a suffocating reinforcement of conformity this was. Not for most people,
since they were not really independent minded individuals with any
distinct personality that would even be capable of feeling smothered.
But a few of us were different. We were secret rebels, and we had to
work hard to compartmentalize our psyche so that we would not be
identified and called out as "deviants." This mental compartmentaliza-
tion only served to intensify and deepen our subversive individuality.

Anna – I mean Marjâna — took me back to her village with her.
Now, visiting such a place was highly questionable for a citizen. They
lived like troglodytes, in a honeycomb of dimly lit chambers roughly
hewn out of a mountainside. It is there that I beheld the living conditions of those who worked deep in the mines, including the ones
where radium was mined to paint our phosphorescent stone 'lights'
and the dials inside our submarines and aerospace craft. They had
cancer from routinely inhaling and handling radioactive dust. Of

course, they didn't know what cancer was. Neither did Marjâna, until I explained it to her. Some of them were frail, with their hair falling out. I'll never forget her holding one man's bald and weary head in her hands as his face twisted in agony while looking up at me as he lay in her lap. It was as if he was trying to form a question to which no one in his benighted world would ever be given an answer. There was something about her posture as she held him that reminded me of a deer, or maybe a gazelle. Marjâna would get a look in her eyes sometimes that made me worry that she would bolt – from me, from this whole unbearable life.

So I tried to expand her horizon. Once, I misappropriated an aerospace craft to give her a view of the Earth from orbit. I can't say that I stole it, because it was 'mine' — to the limited extent that anyone had personal property in this society. But it was strictly forbidden for anyone but full-blooded citizens to leave the surface of the Earth, or for that matter, to travel beneath the surface of the oceans in our submarines. Her wide eyes were unforgettable. She looked down, astonished, then looked back at me with the wonder of a little girl, and then out the cockpit window again, and then back at me. I smiled, with tears in my eyes. "This is *your* world," I said.

As we descended toward the city again, others like it could be seen amidst the dense forests of the vast continental island with its soaring snow-capped mountains — the Transantarctic mountains of today. The cities were few and far between, encircled by a wilderness teeming with beasts like saber-tooth tigers and mammoths grazing on the plains. Each of the cities was heavily fortified against the savage world outside its high walls. The polygonal megalithic construction of these walls went back to the days when such a fortification had to be strong enough to keep out small bands of surviving dinosaurs. These "dragons" had by and large been hunted to extinction by now, especially the ones who could fly over the walls to threaten the city's livestock from above. The few that endured had been cowered into keeping their distance from civilization. It was becoming increasingly

difficult to maintain the heroic tradition of going into the wilderness
to slay a dragon as an initiatory right of passage.

Now, what was most menacing in the woodlands, were the ape
men. They were dimwitted and could be easily mesmerized, but when,
occasionally, we failed to bring them under our hypnotic control, these
beasts were capable of a kind of willfully homicidal violence unseen
from any other predatory animal. This life form had been the basis
for the genetic modification, hybridization, and eugenic breeding that
eventually yielded the various quasi-human or humanoid races con-
stituting the castes of any city's ethno-social pyramid. Producing these
humanoid castes from the wild hominids of the woodlands was the
first major project that preoccupied our ancestors when they arrived
as refugees after the cosmic war that rendered the surface of Mars
nearly uninhabitable and evaporated the oceans of our now desiccated
home world.

The more Marjâna saw of our world, and the more I gleaned of
hers, we began to feel as if anything would be preferable to a continu-
ation of this state of affairs. I remember being high up in the stone
tower of my apartment with her, looking out the balcony as the sun set
over the city, and kneeling together in the most profound and focused
prayer. It wasn't just the two of us. Other secret "deviants" were doing
the same. We prayed for a force of nature strong enough to bring the
vampiric immortality of this godforsaken civilization to an end. We
implored nature to turn on the undead master race, wipe clean the
memory of their heavenly heritage and break the chains of history
that destined everyone else to serve them. We begged for Poseidon
or Typhon to baptize the world with a new beginning. But God helps
those who help themselves, so we also began conspiring to use a system of directed energy and telluric resonance amplification for the
purpose of triggering volcanic eruptions, massive earthquakes, and
attendant tsunamis. We hardly expected that this would be so spectacularly successful that the tremors would cause the Earth's entire
crust to slip over its mantle, tossing the oceans out of their basins and

presenting us with the horrific illusion that the stars were suddenly falling in a defiance and derangement of celestial fate.

This made it considerably more difficult to execute the plans that we had made for bringing about a renaissance after the engineered catastrophes. The sites that we had chosen for educating the primitive population were battered by the worldwide flood, and we had to wait for the waters to recede before we could repair the damage and round up enough survivors to begin the process of reconstructing civilization — a new *human* civilization. There were twelve principal sites: two of them in what is now Egypt, at Giza and Abydos, one in contemporary Mexico, one in Bolivia, one in Peru, one in China, one in the part of the Gobi (at that time, not yet a desert) that is currently within Mongolia, a couple in Northern India, and several in the Middle East (one each inside the present borders of Iran, Iraq, and Turkey). Megalithic buildings had been constructed at each of these sites in advance of the artificial cataclysm, and extensive measurements had been made, and ground plans drawn, for many more structures to be built afterwards — including gargantuan pyramids and massive temples aligned with stellar patterns and built in such a way as to mark the equinoxes and solstices.

We had a superbly high-precision long-count zodiacal calendar that had been designed to keep time over the hundreds of years that it took for journeys back and forth between the various inhabited planets of the solar system and beyond. After the cosmic war, what remained of these worlds were largely cut off from each other, but the calendar endured as a legacy of that age when the once verdant surface of Mars was still our homeland. Those cities were tombs now, literally. Some of the leaders were still there on Mars in cryogenic suspension sarcophaguses that had been set up inside the largest pyramids. Little did they know that their side had lost the war and no one would be coming to their titanic bunker to resurrect them. In a sense, they were the silent guardians of the vast archives that had been left behind on that planet. Once, I participated in one of the very few interplanetary missions that were launched with great difficulty in order to retrieve information from these Martian archives. We arrived in the midst of a terrible sandstorm, and all of us were killed. I had to astral project back into one of the clone bodies in my chamber. Marjâna was repulsed by the slight differences in my physiognomy the next time we saw each other, even if the reincarnation also meant a significant increase in my vitality.

You might imagine that when I recounted these memories to Anna, she would think that I had gone insane. But something worse than that happened. She began to have her own recollections of that place. What place? We concurred that it had to be the lost civilization that, in both Russia and the West, has been referred to as "Atlantis" since the time of Plato. We went to the Strand and also a metaphysical bookstore in the village, where we bought numerous volumes on the subject, from the classic *Atlantis, the Antediluvian World* by Ignatius Donnelly to *Atlantis Rising*, which had just been published by a certain Brad Steiger. We scoured the books of Madam Blavatsky, Rudolf Steiner, and Edgar Casey for their references to Atlantis. Anna described her surfacing memories having the quality of something that one struggles to remember from a dream or from the forgotten parts of our early childhood, with no aid from photographs.

Some of her memories were very painful. They were of her life as a courtesan before she met me. When she recounted these to me, I could see why certain members of the governing elite were concerned that having sex slaves would corrupt us. Since I never engaged in such acts as she described, I could not have imagined what they meant by the corruption that these conservatives were concerned about precisely because *they were the ones* being corrupted. Apparently, having absolute power over the body of a woman who was not his own wife brought out the worst in more than one Atlantean man. This was why when she had met me in that life, she was so surprised that I did not treat her how she had, by then, expected to be treated. It is also why, after Marjâna got to know me, and we fell in love, she rarely wanted to have sex. That was fine with me, and truth be told, it felt more erotic to share subversive and mind-expanding secrets with her. But I did not realize how much trauma was behind the fact that she would get uncomfortable if I tried to do anything more than tenderly kiss or hold her. To her, sex had come to mean perverse humiliation and terrifying violence. Not something you do with someone that you love — or see as an angel of redemption.

Anna described how in her life as Marjâna, well, actually, before I gave her that name and she served namelessly, a number of different Atlantean men had badly abused her. The abuse consisted of various forms of sexual perversion, sadism, and occasional masochism — although, after the heat of passion, the latter would always end with a terribly sadistic reassertion of authority and a punishment for having witnessed the man being humiliated (or humiliating himself).

Sometimes this was followed up by torture from the 'proper' wives of these men. Once, one of the wives beat her with a rod, and then, as she lay on the stone floor unable to move, the woman pulled her dress up, squatted over Marjâna's face, and relieved herself. While she was still writhing in the piss and shit, this Atlantean 'lady' grabbed her hair and dragged her out of the room by it with Nordic brutality. Women like that resented her for bearing witness to their husbands shamelessly expressing themselves and indulging desires that were too crude for them to be allowed to experience.

On numerous occasions, she was chained, bound, whipped, and gagged, sometimes by several men at a time, men she believed were simply using her as a prop and an excuse to secretly explore their own deviant homosexuality. For example, when they would rub their cocks together as two or three of them made her give them oral sex simultaneously, or when one fucked her ass while she rode another and sucked the cock of a third man who stood there overlooking the two men — occasionally grabbing them by their hair, when he wasn't slapping her. Like all sex slaves, she had been fitted with a device that prevented her from getting pregnant from all of the sperm that was shot into her, almost as much as she was forced to drink from one cock after another.

Marjâna — I mean Anna — was often in tears telling me these things. She was hardly a prude, but she found it hard to look into my eyes when she shared these surfacing memories. I think what really made her ashamed was that, on some level, reliving these experiences really turned her on. She did not tell me this, but when she would get in the bath I would notice that her discarded panties were soaked through right where her lips were hugging them. She had never gotten that dripping wet with me before, I mean without even being touched or kissed. This was disturbing enough, but before long she stopped wanting to have sex with me. I never felt comfortable pushing her, especially since she had gone from being capable of multiple orgasms in all the years we made love to not being able to climax no matter how hard I fucked her or how long I went down on her. She started getting really drunk at night, before we would go to bed together. Then, there would be days when I'd come home from the World Trade Center, and she would still be out — long after her day classes were over at the New School. Sometimes, when she would get home, Anna would go straight into the shower. She liked to soak in baths, but on these occasions she would take a quick shower.

Finally, I confronted her. Passionate Russians that we were, we had our share of heated arguments through the years, but this fight was the worst. While she was in the shower, I had discovered cocaine dusted all over the inside of her handbag, together with a pair of panties that she had taken off because they were full of sperm. I wondered why she hadn't just thrown them out on the way home. It was as if she had wanted to get caught. Maybe she wished that I would punish her. She threw her high-heeled shoes at me. Then, although she was evidently already drunk, Anna poured herself vodka on the rocks with a lit cigarette dangling from her pursed lips. A half hour and two drinks later, she hurled that glass across the room at me. I ducked and it shattered on the wall.

I ran after her as she went toward the terrace, threatening to throw herself off the edge of the building. I tackled her to the carpeted floor of the living room, and then she tried hard to choke me. After grabbing her wrists to release her grip on my neck, I finally smacked her once across the face. She screamed through her tears: "Hit me! Hit me again!!!" I slapped her one more time, fairly lightly, but horrified at myself nonetheless. "Harder!!! Please," she cried. Then she reached for my pants and tried frantically to open them. Her bathrobe had already slipped open from the struggle. "Fuck me!" she screamed. "Can't you just fuck me!?!?"

I pulled her hands off the crotch of my pants, and slipped down to embrace her body with my head on her abdomen. "Please, please," she whimpered. From the way her stomach muscles reverberated, I could tell that she was silently weeping. Then, it was not so silent. I pulled myself back up over her and looked down into the most tortured and despairing expression that I've ever seen on a human face. That was with her eyes closed. When she opened them to look at me, so briefly before she turned away, I could see searing shame.

"You don't have to be ashamed," I said softly, "just talk to me. It's ok, you can tell me anything. Please, tell me what's been going on." She responded to my reassuring voice by weeping uncontrollably, tilting her head back and looking at the terrace again, toward the ledge of which she also reached with each of her arms before I took her hands into mine and caressed them. "Just kill me," she pleaded.

It was a long time before Anna calmed down enough to talk coherently. She sat next to me in our bed, and confessed everything. Before finding what ultimately forced me to confront her I feared that maybe she had been having an affair, but no. It wasn't like that. Anna hadn't been passionately seduced into infidelity by some dream lover, or fallen in love with a man other than me. She had become a prostitute.

Now, understand, at that time I still had considerable inherited wealth and not only did I support her, I lavishly spent my money getting her everything that she even showed the slightest hint of desiring.

No, she was not prostituting herself for want of money. She wanted to be degraded, abused, humiliated, and made filthy by the men who fucked her. One of the reasons she wouldn't let me have sex with her anymore is that she was having unprotected sex with them. She had an IUD, so she didn't need to worry about pregnancy, but she let herself be exposed to any disease that they might have. With her head buried in her hands, pulling away as I tried to put my arm around her, she admitted that on some days, instead of going to class, she would try to find three or four different men to cum in her. She didn't care much whether it was in her pussy, her mouth or her ass. She just wanted to be defiled.

I asked her whether she enjoyed any of this masochism, if she got pleasure out of it, or was just torturing herself. She crumpled down into a fetal position and turned away from me. I pulled her onto my lap, and wiped the tears from her cheeks. "It's ok. Tell me." She admitted to having the most intense orgasms of her life. Sometimes several of them at a time. If some pathetic man prematurely ejaculated and left her unsatisfied, she would be sure to find another to fuck her brains out the same day.

It was not hard to understand what had happened. Marjâna's memories had been integrated by Anna to the point that they became her own, thereby deeply restructuring her personality from out of parts of her that had been locked in her subconscious. They hadn't been fully integrated, though. She was only half conscious when she prostituted herself. It was clear to me, from what she was describing, that Anna was in a quasi-mesmeric state when she did these things. It was almost as if Marjâna was doing them, with Anna's body. But there was more to it than a sense of not being able to help herself. She had come to deeply resent me, at least on a subconscious level. I was no longer just Nikolai to her. Now, I was also Dârâ-El, the Atlantean.

This man had been her master, in a society where she was a slave — a sex slave. It is true that he — rather, I — never abused her and was so determined to liberate her and others like her, that I was willing to commit the highest treason imaginable by collaborating in the deliberate destruction of Atlantis. Still, I had been her *master* and heir to a civilization that was not even of this world, one transplanted from the dead planet Mars — a civilization that not only enslaved her kind, but that *created* her kind, humankind, as a race of biological robots who were never supposed to evolve into conscious and conscientious individuals.

Now that she was reintegrating her memories of having been Marjâna, Anna held my Atlantean heritage against me. She didn't mean to, but she did. On the one hand her having sex with these random men rather than me was a sign of reverence, of seeing me as too sacred to defile, and on the other hand it was a punishment driven by vengeful resentment over implicit oppression — implicit in the sense that even my benevolence as a rebel Atlantean was a tacit reaffirmation of her inferiority, of her being at my mercy. These two convoluted motivations for her prostitution were inextricably conflated.

What made things a lot worse was the fact that my day job consisted of remote viewing what appeared to be *survivors from Atlantis*, and *not* ones aligned with those of us who went around the world on a mission of consciousness-raising and the enlightenment of humanity (really, in a sense, the creation of true "humanity"). Rather, the occulted undersea and subterranean civilization that I had described to Anna from the beginning of my work for Naval Intelligence (yes, in violation of my secrecy oath) was clearly constituted by the Atlantean old guard. Their mission was to *restore* as much as they could of the Atlantean society that we had sought to destroy. They would never be able to regress the majority of contemporary humanity back into the mesmerized slaves that they had once been, but they could come as close as possible by using new technologies and techniques of control to force people back into a caste system with themselves at the top of it. One thing that I had learned during my sessions atop the World Trade Center was that this Atlantean Underworld had created European Fascism and, especially, German National Socialism, as a vehicle for a restoration of Atlantis. They saw the Nazis, particularly the SS, as *Kshatriyas* who would build a pyramid for them to ascend as the *Brahmins* of a New World Order.

This meant that Anna could not even take comfort in the trauma of her life as Marjâna being something suffered in the distant past. The 'people' who had visited that suffering upon her were alive and well, planning their reemergence with the patience of titans, each of whose lives span thousands of our years, and who have total recall from one incarnation to the next. She resented me for just watching them, day in and day out, without doing anything to stop them. Anna even suspected that the purpose of the sessions was really to seduce me into collaborating with this Underworld, or with the post-war Fascist shadow government that is facilitating their machinations. It is not as if that thought had never occurred to me. I had suppressed this suspicion, but when Anna confessed that it was one of the factors motivating her extremely destructive behavior, I had to face it forthrightly. I needed to know. Was I being used? By whom? For how long? To what end? Tragically, Anna would not live to see me answer those agonizing questions.

One day, I came back home from work to find Anna missing. She had stopped prostituting herself for some time, so I was really worried. My intuition was that she was in real danger. In just the past couple of days, she had finally been able to surrender to total intimacy with me again. The first time that she climaxed with me since being overcome by memories of our life in Atlantis, her moans of ecstasy quickly turned into hysterical weeping. She could barely look at me, and when I gently compelled her to do so I saw overwhelming sadness, shame, and regret in her eyes. The next day we were closer than we had ever been.

I try to console myself with the thought that when I wrapped my arms around her from behind, breathing her hair, as she stood in the kitchen stirring her coffee with downcast eyes, she could feel my unequivocal forgiveness and renewed adoration of her. That night, when we made love again, I implored her to keep looking into my eyes. She did, although I had to keep wiping the tears off her cheeks, which were covered with smeared mascara by the time she came. Then, looking up at me as if she would not see me again for a long time, she held my head in her hands as I let go. I wish I had understood that expression then, and I'll never forgive myself for going to work the next morning.

Throughout the evening and into the night, as I paced frantically while waiting for her to come home, I kept getting terrible flashes of her alone on a beach, crying and playing chicken at the ocean's edge with waves crashing from out of the darkness. I felt like I was suffocating. My every impulse was to go out looking for Anna, to follow these impressions to Coney Island and scour the beach in search of her. But I was held back by the fear that she would finally come home, already so deeply distressed, and find me gone. It was possible that the images coming to me were only symbolic. How would I know where to look for her?

The next morning I went to the police. They told me that she hadn't been missing for long enough to justify their doing anything about it. So I asked Jack for a favor. I knew I was too involved to trust the objectivity of any clairvoyant impressions of my own, so I explained as much of the situation to him as he needed to know before requesting that two other remote viewers be tasked — off the record — to find my Anna. As per usual protocol, they wouldn't need to know what or who the target was. Only Jack would know when he analyzed their independently obtained data. He agreed. Aware of the urgency of the situation, Jack had both of these men do sessions on the same day, and by early evening he was grimly comparing the notes and sketches made by them. After making the request in person that morning, I had gone back home to be there in case Anna returned, even though, in the pit of my stomach, I knew that she wasn't coming back.

Jack called me around sunset, and asked if he could come over. I met him in the long hallway of the lobby. He had the gravest look that I'd ever seen on his face. Considering his personality, it was quite startling. He had a leather dossier holder under his arm. We didn't exchange a word in the elevator and he tried to avoid eye contact.

Without his needing to request it, I poured him a glass of scotch and made another one for myself. My hands were shaking as I tried to get the ice cubes out of the tray. He sat on the sofa in my living room sipping his scotch a few times, before opening the leather portfolio. Jack sighed as he laid the papers inside it across my sofa. Then he sat back, and glanced across at me. I was leaning forward in my armchair. "She's dead, Nick. She drowned herself. Brighton Beach."

Silence. Dead silence. I'd say I could hear my heartbeat, but I felt like my heart had stopped. I couldn't breathe. I didn't even bother to look at the papers. When I managed to form words again, I asked, "where's her body?" Jack pressed his fingers into his forehead, covering his eyes with his hand, with his head downcast. "It'll wash up on the beach," he said.

What if she had no identification on her? How was I supposed to go to the police and ask them to keep an eye out for the corpse of a "Jane Doe" to wash up on the beach? Jack said that he would take care of it, and that he would also make the funeral arrangements for me. I explained to him that Anna was totally alienated from her family, and that she had few friends who would show up to any funeral. I wanted her cremated, and to keep her urn by my side, but only after I got to see her body one last time.

Jack came through. He had a Navy Seal Team retrieve Anna's corpse from Brighton Beach before it was even discovered by the police, and before the seagulls could disfigure her too badly. Part of me died forever when I stood over her lifeless body at the morgue. The morticians had been instructed by Naval Intelligence not to ask too many questions. She was cremated, and the urn of her ashes became my most cherished possession. It was not gaudy gold, but black and embossed with the Trident of Poseidon.

CHAPTER 5

FAUSTIAN BARGAIN

After Anna's suicide, answering the question that she had forced me to formulate in full consciousness became an all consuming quest. Despite how helpful Jack was in dealing with her death, I could not put him above the suspicion of being party to a vast conspiracy to manipulate me. There was the danger that indulging such conspiratorial suspicions was a sign of encroaching paranoia, which from a psychoanalytic standpoint would be considered an "understandable" reaction to all that I had been through in the mere 27 years of my life. But I knew better. Archontic forces were at work weaving this tangled web, whose strands included the gruesome death of my parents, trauma-induced paranormal ability, recruitment into the intelligence field as a psychic spy, and the suicide of my beloved. It was the Spring of 1974 when I began investigating the misfortunes of my life. In hindsight, it was like being a detective endeavoring to discover *in advance* who and what *would be* responsible for the crime of one's own untimely demise.

I decided to begin at the beginning. Nostalgic and sentimental as I am, I had carefully kept almost all of my aunt's personal belongings boxed up in my closets or in the storage of our building. I went through all of these things looking for some clue. It was not long before I happened upon a set of old photographs of what, on the face of it, was my father and mother. One might assume that it was my mother, because the body language between her and my father bespoke an intimacy that is exclusive to longtime lovers. Also, my 'uncle' supposedly hated my father "the communist" to the extent that he forbade her from visiting her own sister who was so contemptible as to marry such a man.

This set of photographs showed my father from long after my uncle married my aunt. He was standing in a wooded area, apparently target practicing, but also mischievously engaging in horseplay with the woman in the photograph. Here is the problem. The woman is brandishing weapons. Proudly holding a sniper rifle, aiming a pistol, and holding a hunting knife to my father's throat with a darkly playful look on her face. I recognized that look. My mother, Marianna, would *never* even have gone *near* any of these weapons. I can't even imagine her firing a gun. This woman *was her identical twin*, namely my aunt Nikita!

What was she doing with my father? Well, obviously, paramilitary training of some kind. They were wearing camouflage outfits, and in some of the pictures a patch with an insignia could be made out on them: a sun wheel whose twelve spokes each extended out to become a bolt of lightning. There was also a pin fastened to each side of the fabric epaulettes of these fatigues, with one star on either side of the pin. But, I mean, what was she *doing* with him, especially given the story I had been told by my uncle?! No wonder my aunt implied that she knew hidden truths about my father. It was obvious from these photographs that they had been comrades and lovers. I shuddered. For years, I had been fucked by my father's lover.

As I mentioned earlier, I was fairly talented at drawing. So I carefully reproduced the symbol on the patch of their grey uniforms, together with the design of the pin on the shoulder bands. I took these drawings to a military historian whose antique shop in Midtown Manhattan I had visited with Anna a few times. He remembered, and asked about her. I did not get into details, but told him that she had died tragically. I could have just lied and made small talk, but it was a good thing that I said this much because it put him in a more caring and concerned mindset. Otherwise, he might have thrown me out of his store or alerted the authorities after looking at my drawings.

When I set them in front of him, he stared wide-eyed at them for a moment with a look of consternation in his face. You see, he was a Ukrainian Jew. He breathed deeply as he took his spectacles off and laid them on the table with a poise that suggested he was struggling to suppress an angry outburst. Then, he looked penetratingly into my eyes, and asked, "Why have you drawn Neo-Nazi symbols?" I said, "What?!" He explained, "these symbols, one is wolf's hook, the other is clever combination of Black Sun with SS lightning bolts."

The anger in his face disappeared, and was replaced by bewildered concern, when he realized that I had no idea what he was talking about. "Where did you see these, young man? Where you draw this from?" When I remained silent, he added, "These symbols today are only used by Neo-Nazis. The *wolfsangel*, this was runic symbol of insurgency against American and Russian occupation of Germany in 1945. The werewolves. This other one, it is invented. But I recognize elements. It is Black Sun, symbol on floor of Wewelsburg Castle of Himmler's knights, but the sun rays, you see, have been drawn like the lightning bolts of SS insignia. You know, SS lightning bolts?" He got up and brought over a black *sig*-rune emblazoned SS flag from his collection of World War II memorabilia. As I was staring at it, dazed, trying to contemplate the implications of all this, he also brought over a wolf's hook pin from one of his glass cases.

I had to quickly think of a constructive lie. "Mr. Lubetkin," I started. He interrupted, "please, Yuri." I claimed that I had seen these symbols spray-painted on walls here in the city. Leaning in and whispering, I told part of the truth (enough of it to get fired), "I work for the government now. We are secretly investigating the people who made this graffiti. Do you know where I could find them?" He sat back in his chair, and looked me over with curiosity and skepticism. "You have badge, young man?" I reached for my wallet, "I'm not supposed to show you this, so please, don't mention to *anybody* that I was here asking questions." I pulled out my access badge for the facility in the World Trade Center. "You are Navy Intelligence?!"

I motioned for him to lower his voice as I nervously looked around the large store from the desk in the back where we were sitting. There was only one other person in there, toward the front. He nodded affirmatively, then motioned for me to wait a minute while he got up and fetched something. It was a contact and address book, crammed with receipts. "These scum, they come here and buy paraphernalia from me. They pretend just interested in make collection from war history. But *I know*. They are Neo-Nazi. Hair cut, military style. Never they make small talk with me. Never eye contact." He opened the book up to a certain page and pulled out a few receipts, setting them to the side of it.

"You mean, like skinheads?" He shook his head violently. "No, more serious. Always they wear three-piece suit. Impeccably dressed, with silk scarf you know. Look like old-style Italian fascists." The pages that he had opened to, and that he now turned toward me, were full of handwritten addresses. Now, *he* leaned in to whisper to *me*, with a twinkle in his eyes. "I have — I had — them followed. *This* one apartment house. *This* one *coffee shop*, where they meet. *That* one bookstore." This old antique dealer and amateur buff of military history turned out to be a Nazi hunter. "My brother," he said with downcast eyes, "he died in Dachau." Then he pulled up the sleeve of his sweater and unbuttoned the wrist of his shirt, exposing the number tattooed on his forearm. "I survived, in Auschwitz."

I tried the coffee shop first, because it was the easiest place to linger in on a regular basis. Then I started frequenting the bookstore. I considered staking out the apartment house, keeping my eye out for especially well-dressed men with fascistic haircuts. But before I had to resort to the latter, they showed up in the coffee shop. After they left, I asked to have a word with the manager. I pulled my badge out again, in total disregard of the consequences for my position with Naval Intelligence. Sufficiently impressed, he asked the waitress who had been serving their table to come talk to me. She very uncomfortably informed me that they were regulars, and, when pressed, gave me an idea of what days and times they tended to frequent the establishment. After a couple of misses, at one of these indicated times I arrived to find them there and got a booth next to theirs. Overhearing their conversation, I was able to conclude that the most senior member of the group of three or four men who would get together there was a corporate executive who also did work as a publisher or publicist.

Shortly thereafter, I saw the same man check one of the shelves in the bookstore, and then go into its backroom to talk to the store's owner. I did not linger long enough for him to notice me, but I came back and carefully looked through the particular bookshelf that he had been searching. That section of this obscure bookshop featured books from the Traditionalist school of Philosophy, with which I was only vaguely familiar at the time. Most of the writings of René Guénon and Julius Evola were there. But what was most interesting was the tome that I had noticed that man pull out before going into the back room. It had a very dramatic red, white, and black cover, with hands clasped over a downward pointing sword, which made me think of Arthur's Excalibur. The title was *Imperium* and the spine identified it as the work of "Ulick Varange." The back cover, however, clarified that this was a pen name used by one Francis Parker Yockey, whose photograph was printed above a brief biography ending with his death in prison in 1960. The picture on the back cover showed him in handcuffs. I bought the book.

Imperium was a shocking read. In this self-described sequel to Oswald Spengler's *Decline of the West*, Yockey (aka. "Varange") argued that after the defeat suffered by Fascism in 1945, the decline of "Faustian civilization" that Spengler analyzed in the 1920s had entered a terminal phase. An even more unapologetically imperial form of totalitarianism would now be necessary to resurrect the dying European world. What was most startling about the thesis of *Imperium* was its valorization of the Soviet Union over the United States. One would think that Fascists would see Communist Russia as their ultimate enemy, and, especially given how many Nazi scientists were imported by America, and how racist the South had remained despite attempted desegregation, the United States would be viewed more favorably by them. But that is not how Yockey saw things. He preferred Stalinism to democratic American "degeneracy" and hoped for the Russians to defeat the United States, in its current form as a capitalist liberal democracy, if only to catalyze the rise of a Fourth Reich — a pan-European "Imperium" — from out of the ruins of the postwar Anglo-American order.

After wrapping my mind around this thesis, I went back to that bookstore and my eye was drawn toward *Men Among the Ruins* by Julius Evola, which forwarded a similar argument. Then I read his *Revolt Against the Modern World*, and Evola's references in that magnum opus led me to the works of Réne Guénon, especially *Crisis of the Modern World* and *The Reign of Quantity*. I took extensive notes on these books. While reading them over, a diabolical idea occurred to me. I would write a book in the vein of these works, so that I could have an excuse to approach the publisher and others in his circle here in New York. But I needed to be able to devote my time to this project in a serious way. So I contrived to disguise my work as research for a doctoral thesis that would critique Traditionalist Fascism.

For the last two years, I had held up my plans to further my graduate studies in Philosophy beyond an MA and in pursuit of a PhD. Before being sent to Jack's office by Hal, I had been thinking to expand my MA thesis into a dissertation. I set this aside now, and decided that after receiving my doctorate I could publish a slightly expanded version of the MA thesis as my second book. My first book would be written under a penname, as Yockey had written his, and it would be written parallel to a doctoral dissertation that afforded me the time to research it. My angle for proposing the PhD thesis would be to argue that 1920s and 30s European Fascism was internally incoherent, strained between opposed polarities of Traditionalism (Guénon, Evola, and Hitler) and Futurism (Nietzsche, Jünger, Marinetti, and to an extent Mussolini). Secretly, the research for this thesis would fuel the writing of a treatise that I planned to title *Faustian Futurism*.

An Iranian-born Professor at the New School would be integral to helping me develop the project. Fereidoun M. Esfandiary had by then conceptualized the characteristics of a new type of Futurists, people who he called "Up Wingers." These were visionary individuals who defied the typical Left/Right political binary, but not by being centrist. Up-Wingers recognized that the radical transformation of human society, toward something that Esfandiary liked to call a "Transhuman" (rather than Superhuman) condition, required social and political structures that could not be neatly categorized as entirely left wing or right wing.

Despite working on what he called "A Futurist Manifesto," Esfandiary did not seem that keen on the history of Futurism or of Faustian European philosophy in general. He had only a superficial familiarity with Nietzsche, and as far as I could tell, had not read Heidegger. But what I wanted to appropriate from Esfandiary, who envisioned a world very much like that depicted in the concept drawings of Syd Mead, was the idea of a radical, revolutionary socio-political vision that was 180 degrees opposite to centrism. Rather than being a compromise between Socialism and Conservatism or Democracy and Totalitarianism, it represented a convergence of opposed polarities at a point beyond their extremes.

On this view, the socio-political spectrum was not just a shoehorn but actually a circle, and there was a position on it diametrically opposite to the moderate center, a position to the Left of Marx and to the Right of Mussolini. Of course, F.M. 2030 would never have put it this way himself. But my argument was going to be that such a position was not only implicit to *his* "Transhuman" Neo-Futurism, it was already there in the Fascist Futurism of 1909–1945. This kind of Fascism was in as much tension with 'Fascist' Traditionalism as it was with Liberal Democracy or a Social Democracy headed toward Communism. In fact, in some ways, it had more in common with the Promethean aspects of Soviet Communism than it did with Traditionalism.

At the core of *Faustian Futurism*, there was to be a contemplation of the bargain that Goethe has his tragic figure of Faust strike with Mephistopheles. Faust makes this promise to the devil, "*Werd ich zum Augenblicke sagen: Verweile doch! Du bist so shön! Dann magst du mich in Fesseln schlagen, Dann will ich gern zugrunde gehn!*" "If I should say to the moment: But tarry! You are so beautiful! Then you might as well bind me in chains, then I will gladly go to my demise!" As Spengler understood when he characterized the West as "Faustian Civilization", this devil's pact is meant to symbolize an ethos of unappeasable striving. Goethe grasped this well, from within himself.

Mephistopheles:
Who could divine toward what you aspire?
It must have been sublimely bold, in truth,
Toward the moon you'd soar and ever higher;
Did your mad quest allure you there forsooth?

Faust:
By no means! For this earthly sphere
Affords a place for great deeds ever.
Astounding things shall happen here,
I feel the strength for bold endeavor.

Mephistopheles [still jeering and skeptical]:
So you'd earn glory? One can see
You've been in heroines' company.

Faust:
Lordship, possession, are my aim and thought!

The will to reach the Moon, already intuited here by the devil, is only another expression of Faustian man's uniquely exploratory spirit. For the sake of writing *Faustian Futurism*, I researched the history of exploration. What I found, and presented in the manuscript, was shocking. But it was sure to appeal to Thompson and his circle. As it turns out, when one defines "the explorer" as a distinct category that is not to be confused with conquerors who crossed vast swathes of land, such as Genghis Khan (or Alexander), one finds that there are only about 15 non-European men out of a total number of approximately 300 explorers in recorded human history. These explorers include naval navigators who sailed previously uncharted seas, and thereby discovered new lands, mountain climbers who scaled peaks, the vistas of which had never been beheld by anyone before them, as well as those individuals who led expeditions to conquer the poles of the Earth, both in the Arctic and Antarctica. Whether these men were ancient Greeks, with their extraordinary maritime culture, or the Vikings who made it to America long before Christopher Columbus, or Renaissance Italians such as Amerigo Vespucci, after which "America" was named, Portuguese and Spanish merchants, British mountain climbers in Africa and India, Germans in the jungles of the Amazons or the Himalaya mountains, or their Germanic kindred in Scandinavia who braved the Antarctic and named large swaths of the frozen continent — they were almost all white men.

What I argued in *Faustian Futurism* was that this was entirely inextricable from the incomparable accomplishment of whites — European and American — in the arts, literature, the sciences and technological innovation. For example, from out of painters and other visual artists of which we have any historical records, whether in Western, Islamic, Indian, or Asian histories, 479 were Westerners as compared to a total of 293 from all non-Western cultures combined (the total population of which far exceeds that of the West, meaning that the 479 Western artists represent a much larger percentage of the population of their own civilization and not just of the world at large). When it comes to great works of literature, 835 Western writers penned works that became historic whereas East Asia, India, and the Muslim world taken together only produced 293 notable authors (again, despite having a much larger combined population than Europe and its colonial territories in the Americas). The imbalance is even more significant in music, although harder to compare with any precision, since non-Western cultures do not even have a tradition of music composition with identifiable individual composers (at least not until they were Westernized very late into modernity).

Finally, as far as science and technology are concerned, "white supremacy" is undisputed. Even when taking the considerable accomplishments of the "Islamic Golden Age" into account, where it must be admitted that 90% of the scientists and inventors were Persians who at that time (800–1100) were still genetically (and not just linguistically) Indo-European, we still arrive at the conclusion that 97% of techno-scientific achievements in history are by white men — whether in Europe, North America, or Russia. This does not include the negligible number of Jews, whose contributions, especially in late modernity, are always overstated.

What is also evident from this statistical analysis, which was laid out in detail in *Faustian Futurism* and which I am only summarizing here, is that IQ is only one part of this puzzle when it comes to comprehending the excellence of Faustian man. It should go without saying that, with an IQ that is in some cases 20 to 30 points below that of Westerners, the native peoples of Africa, Arabia, and India (as compared to the small Aryan minority who brought higher culture there) could not possibly hope to compete with Faustian man in any area of human achievement. However, the Chinese have a very high average IQ, comparable to the most intelligent Western populations, but as can be seen most clearly in their attempts at exploration, they lack all of the other personality traits that account for Faustian achievement. What one gleans from the chronicles of the voyages of Cheng Ho, and the burning of the Chinese ships that may have made it to the Americas, is a terror in the face of the unknown and its potential for destabilization of society. "May you live in interesting times," is a Chinese curse.

The Chinese fear of change, which is bound up with their ancestor worship, filial piety, collectivism, and conformism, precluded Chinese greatness in every domain of human achievement dominated by Westerners—including scientific discovery and technological innovation—*despite their comparable* mathematical and spatial reasoning capacity. *Faustian Futurism* argued that while the Chinese do not suffer from some of the genetic deficits that prevented other ethnic groups from rivaling the West in achievement, such as the poor impulse control of Africans or the undisciplined and unfocused laziness of Arabs in the Islamic World and the Dravidian majority in India, on a population-wide level the Chinese—despite their discipline and focus—lack the genetic predisposition to bold inquisitiveness, curiosity to the point of dangerous risk taking, iconoclastic individuality, wondrous enjoyment of pure creativity, and a horizon-expanding will to transcend all apparent limitations.

Every moment in the life of a Faustian man is felt to be incomplete as compared to an imagined moment of greater fulfillment. Heidegger is only reiterating this when, in *Being and Time*, he offers an analysis of temporality that describes existence as ever incomplete and always oriented toward a future from out of which the present secondarily takes shape, through an appropriation (or misappropriation) of the past. Western man is ceaselessly driven beyond himself, as restless as a vampire in the night of time.

The Heideggerian "homelessness of Dasein" is also an ethno-linguistic echo of the fact that Goethe's Faust feels as if he is a vagabond and *unbehause*—a "homeless person"—incapable of ever happily abiding in the world or belonging to any place that would be his own. This is the reason why the fifth and final act of Part II of *Faust* ends with the protagonist ordering Mephistopheles and his gang of devils to immolate Philemon and Baucis together with their home that, in the original telling of their tale by Ovid, had become a temple for Jupiter and Mercury. This elderly couple, who refuse forced resettlement, stood in the way of the completion of Faust's vast techno-scientific, political, and economic engineering project. Philemon and Baucis represent gratitude to the gods for the blessedness of the present moment. The transformation of their home into a temple signifies a sanctification of hospitality that presupposes this world can be hospitable — albeit under the roof of reverence for the God-Father and his errand boy. In league with the devil, Faust incinerates the house of this world's hospitality.

I had no trouble being admitted to the PhD program in the Philosophy department at the New School, especially since I was not asking for funding. What was more challenging was resigning from Naval Intelligence. When I broke it to Jack, I laid emphasis on my psychological distress over Anna's suicide. In fact, I had missed many days at work, and it was no lie that my mental state was deteriorating and I was increasingly unable to focus on the task at hand there, especially since what I was remote viewing had a direct bearing on Anna's having drowned in our shared memories of Atlantis.

Jack agreed to grant me a "temporary leave." His insistence that I maintain my security clearance seemed to me to be a way of keeping a fishhook in me — or maybe it was a wolf's hook. After all, that's what I was out to find out. Who really wanted me immersed, on a daily basis, in a clairvoyance of the Atlantean Underworld, and *why*? Was I being initiated into a Traditionalist cabal that had managed to infiltrate parts of the American intelligence community? Before going back to work at the Twin Towers, I needed to know. Anna was intensely intuitive. Had she been onto some unbearable secret about me? A secret about my tortured life that even I had no *conscious* access to.

Within nine months of leaving Naval Intelligence and beginning my doctoral studies in Philosophy at the New School, I had a working draft of *Faustian Futurism*. I wrote that draft like a madman in Frankenstein's laboratory, hammering away on my typewriter through many long nights. I had enough to approach the publisher. Meanwhile, I also managed to follow him to his corporate office at 16 East 52nd Street. I had a word with the security guard, who proved to be easier to prevail upon than I could have imagined. He assumed that I was from the FBI, since apparently the Feds were also carrying out clandestine surveillance of this man. His name was Harold Keith Thompson, and one wintery day in early 1975 I was headed up to his office, typed and bound manuscript in hand, dressed in the same impeccable manner as was customary for him and his Fascist associates.

When I stepped out of the elevator, I saw that Thompson was well protected. There was a secretary up front and the place was walled off in a way that offered no direct access to his office. An envelope with a letter in it was paper-clipped to the manuscript, which I left with his secretary. She asked, "Is he expecting it?" I lied, "Yes, miss." I also gave her my phone number and my real name, as opposed to the pen name, "Nick Griffin," which appeared on the manuscript's title page. Within five days I got a phone call from the same secretary, who set up an appointment for one week from the evening that she contacted me. I assumed, rightly it turned out, that this meant Thompson had started reading the draft of *Faustian Futurism* with interest and wanted to finish it before meeting with me.

What I could not have been prepared for is the reception I was given when I walked into Thompson's office. He was a hard man, of stoic Northern European demeanor, with a clean cut long face and closely trimmed dark hair. I had hardly seen a smile when I spied on the conversations he had with his associates at the coffee shop. But the icy stoicism of his full lips broke into an irrepressible smile as he saw me appear in the open doorway across from his desk. He did not get up, but he gestured for me to sit in the chair across from him. I smiled back and extended my hand to shake his as I took my seat, hoping to feign a calm confidence. He had a wicked look in his eyes as he shook my hand, and then grabbed it for a moment longer as I attempted to release my grip.

"Welcome home, Nick." He saw how speechlessly disconcerted I was by this greeting, wondering whether he meant it only metaphorically, as an indication of how much he identified with what I had written in the manuscript. "You don't remember me, do you? Of course, you don't. You were just a boy. A very shy boy, as I recall." Then, slowly, terribly as fate, it started to come back to me. Yes, I *had* seen this man before. He was one of the 'gentlemen' sitting around our dining table at one of the soirées that I witnessed in the first year, or maybe even the first few months, after I had moved in with my aunt and uncle. He was about 20 years younger then, but he hadn't changed all that much.

"My god," I couldn't stop myself from mumbling under my breath. "Did you know my aunt?" I asked. He sneered. "Did I *know* her?! We called her *mother*. She *led* us, Nick. Until she was burdened with the responsibility of actually being a mother to you. She took that very seriously, and we stopped seeing much of her." He picked up the manuscript of *Faustian Futurism*, "I see she raised you well." Now he got up to pour us drinks from the decanter of scotch to the side of his desk. "Let's drink to that."

What was I going to do? I felt like I had stumbled into a den of wolves, and that the only way I was going to survive was to pretend to be one of them. Moreover, I now knew beyond denial that the woman who had raised me, the sorceress who had initiated me, was the she-wolf at the head of this pack. I proposed a toast to Nikita, and we sipped scotch together.

"You know what happened to my aunt?" He nodded gravely. "She could never get over the death of your father," he said. "He was good friends with Yockey, your father was." While trying to process the shock of learning that the author of *Imperium* had been a personal friend of my father, I retained enough mental focus to pointedly ask, "Over the death of *my father*? What about the murder of *her sister*?!" He gave me a hard stare while swirling the whiskey in his glass.

There was a long silence. "My mother…" I started to say again. Thompson looked at me a little bit like one looks pitifully at a witless man. I felt 'reality' giving way under my feet right there in that office. He cut in before I could embarrass myself, "Listen, kid, I know you had a hard life. But what doesn't kill you, makes you stronger, and judging by what you've written here, you've become very strong indeed."

"So you'll publish it," I said, a little too hesitantly. "You better believe it, kid! Not only am I going to publish it, I want to introduce you to someone who will ensure that this masterpiece makes it to all the right people." I strained to keep a poker face. "Michel d'Obrenovic. But you wouldn't know him under that name, because we asked him to write all of his books under a pen name. Ever heard of George Hunt Williamson?" I nodded that I had. Williamson had been a member of the infamous contactee George Adamski's inner circle, before the two had a falling out and Williamson formed his own flying saucer cult with a group of fellow occultists. He was best known for *The Saucers Speak*. I had happened upon his books back when I was digging up everything I could about Atlantis. A number of his books, such as *Secret Places of the Lion* and *Secret of the Andes* had archeological themes involving ancient Egypt and Peru, alleging that these civilizations had been established by the "Space Brothers." In 1961, Williamson disappeared and no one, including his numerous followers, had heard a thing from him since then.

Williamson went around calling himself "Doctor", which is how Adamski had referred to him, but it later turned out that his academic credentials were fraudulent. I raised this point with Thompson. He replied, "they weren't faked. His degrees were under his real name, Michel d'Obrenovic, which he's gone back to using now. His doctoral dissertation was on Mayan hieroglyphics. The guy's military credentials were also legitimate, by the way. Again, just not under the name Williamson. D'Obrenovic worked for both the Army and the Navy."

"Why did he pull a disappearing act?" I asked. Thompson smiled smugly as he leaned back in his chair, swirling his scotch again. "Well, he hasn't exactly disappeared. He's just done playing his part as

George Hunt Williamson. Good actor, that guy. Figures that he's been involved with so many dramatists — playwrights, actors, actresses. His second wife, Jennifer Holt, who he just married a couple of years ago, is an actress who's starred in tens of Westerns. They live in Santa Barbara. I want you to go down there and meet with him, after he's had a chance to read this manuscript of yours."

Somehow I muddled through an hour of awkward conversation with Thompson, before hailing the first checkered cab I could find to take me back home. My head was pounding the whole time. I had to roll the windows down. The taxi driver looked at me in the rear view mirror a few times, concerned that I was going to puke all over his back seat. When I finally got home, I collapsed onto that bed that my aunt had seduced me into for all those years after my uncle died. The bed that she had overdosed in, the one that I had bedded Anna in before she was driven to prostitution and suicide.

CHAPTER 6

HOTEL CALIFORNIA

hen I finally woke up, rather than wondering if the whole thing had been a nightmare, it was as if I had awakened from out of life and into an inescapable nightmare. I began to feel like Number 6 when he woke up inside that apartment that was a simulacrum of his own, but built inside The Village. *The Prisoner* starring Patrick McGoohan was one of my favorite shows. I was now convinced that whoever wrote this series knew that there was in fact an occulted third power in the world, an international cabal coveting futuristic technology that allowed it to pursue its own objectives above and beyond the exoteric opposition between the American and Soviet camps. There was even an allusion to UFOs in the form of the "rover" spheres that are launched from out of the water around the secret island, acting as vigilant warders of its prison population consisting of former intelligence agents from both sides of the Cold War.

I began obsessively researching Williamson and his connection with the more infamous Adamski. If I was going to fly out to California to meet this shady character, I figured that I had better know as much as possible about what I was getting myself into. I began with what was publicly available about Adamski before I paid a few visits back to the joint NSA and Naval Intelligence facility at the World Trade

Center, with my still intact security clearance, to unearth some information that is not publicly available — especially about D'Obrenovic.

The first thing that is noteworthy about Adamski, who emigrated with his parents from Poland to New York at two years of age, is that prior to becoming the leader of a Contactee cult, he was the founder of the Royal Order of Tibet in Laguna Beach, California. Here is what the *Los Angeles Times* had to say about the self-styled "Professor" as early as April of 1934. The article is titled "Shamanistic Order to be Established Here" and includes an interview with the guru, who claimed to have studied secret doctrines from the lamas in Tibet:

> The 10-foot trumpets of far away Lhasa, perched among perpetual snows in the Himalayan Mountains in Tibet, will shortly have their echo on the sedate hills of Southern California's Laguna Beach. Already the Royal Order of Tibet has acquired acreage on the placid hills that bathe their Sunkist feet in the purling Pacific and before long, the walls, temples, turrets and dungeons of a Lama monastery will serrate the skyline. It will be the first Tibetan monastery in America and in course of time, the trained disciples of the cult will filter through its glittering gates to spread 'the ancient truths' among all who care to listen. The central figure in the new movement is Professor George Adamski…
>
> "I learned great truths up there on the roof of the world," says Adamski, "or rather the trick of applying age-old knowledge to daily life, to cure the body and the mind, and to win mastery over self and soul. I do not bring to Laguna the weird rites and bestial superstition in which the old Lamaism is steeped, but the scientific portions of the religion."

Six years later Adamski had moved from Laguna Beach to Palomar Mountain, California, the site of what was then one of the greatest observatories in the world. The Polish immigrant was apparently already wealthy enough to have purchased twenty acres of land on the mountain, which he called Palomar Gardens, where he opened up a restaurant. It is here at the Palomar Gardens Café that, in 1946, Adamski was approached by a group of military officers who told him that the UFOs he had recently observed in the area were "not of this world." Interestingly, this was not Adamski's own initial impression. In his first book, *Flying Saucers Have Landed*, published in 1953, Adamski wrote of the first cigar-shaped UFO that he saw in California, "I figured that during the war some new type of aircraft had been developed and that this was one of them." In his second book, *Inside the Spaceships*, which came out two years later in 1955, Adamski offers a cryptic and deeply disturbing remark that suggests this "new type of aircraft" developed during the Second World War was a product of Nazi German engineering:

> National security has many facets and the powers that be are themselves pushing out in the direction of space and of anti-gravity. Also, they know they have an enemy. And they do not know how far the enemy may have gone in this general field of a new form of power and propulsion. They do know that at the close of the war all the German scientists with knowledge did not come to this country.

Adamski is clearly referring to Operation Paperclip here, and letting it be known that he is privy to American military awareness of fugitive Nazi scientists with knowledge of anti-gravity who went elsewhere than to America and who are still considered "an enemy" of the United States. This is just the rim of the rabbit hole. Adamski demonstrates detailed knowledge of a flying saucer's propulsion system, which as I was able to piece together from the information that I had access to at Naval Intelligence, was a system achieved by the Germans at a research facility at Prague in 1944 as part of a "Project Chronos" that was being run by the SS in quest of a "wonder weapon" that was expected to be so "decisive for the war" that it was given the highest classification above Top Secret, higher even than the Nazi Atom Bomb project.

In *Flying Saucers Have Landed*, Adamski describes the saucer's technology as "magnetic", relating that he "noticed two rings under the flange around the center disk. This inner ring between the outer one appeared to be revolving clockwise, while the ring between these two moved in a counter clockwise motion." This kind of electro-magnetic counter-rotation was used by Nazi scientists to spin an isotope of mercury-thorium inside a prototype free energy and anti-gravity device that they had called "the Bell" (*Die Glocke*) on account of the acorn-like shape of its casing. Adamski goes on to describe a "rod of power" with each of its ends anchored to the ceiling and floor by two "great lenses" at the dead center of any one of the flying saucers, which his blond-haired Nordic-looking "Space Brothers" allowed him to board. They explained to Adamski that this was the "magnetic pole" of the craft and that it could interact with the Earth's magnetic field.

Adamski elaborates on this electro-magnetic anti-gravity technology in *Inside the Spaceships*, where he writes that he "was aware of a very slight hum that seemed to come equally from beneath the floor and from a heavy coil that appeared to be built into the top of the circular wall. The moment the hum started, this coil began to glow bright red but emitted no heat." Soon after it began to glow, Adamski heard a sound that he describes as a "soft hum as of a swarm of bees." The Nazi Bell was also called *der Bienenstock* or "the Beehive" on account of exactly this sound that it made as it began to levitate, pulling on the chains that were used to tether the prototype inside a research rig. Adamski's putatively faked photographs of flying saucers happen to be dead ringers for the designs depicted in SS papers that outline Mark I, II, and III Hannebu saucer-shaped craft that the Bell was going to be installed into as a power source and propulsion device.

Adamski claimed that the Space Brothers told him that they would share the technology of gravity control, were it not for the fact that they feared that terrestrial humanity would weaponize it into a kind of electro-magnetic gravity bomb that would produce an implosion far more powerful than a hydrogen bomb explosion. Only they were wise enough to wield this power. In fact, Adamski claimed that they were so wise that they would be capable of solving all of Earth's problems. He told the coterie of cult followers that flocked to him that the beautiful Nordic-looking cigar and saucer pilots had a system of government far more futuristic than that of the United States, one wherein warring nation-states had been done away with, and churches, educational institutions, scientific research, economy and industry had all been centralized under a single government with a spiritual mission, which bound their telepathic society together through a common purpose involving perpetual reincarnation and "spiritual growth through service."

The psychic powers of these Supermen were so great, claimed Adamski, that should they wish to do so they could produce miracles that would awe humanity into submission. For now, they were attempting to use more modest means to persuade the United States to give up its nuclear weapons — which they claimed were harmful to the ecosystem. They had even sent an emissary to the Pentagon to make this demand. Adamski claimed that he was told that they already had 40,000,000 of their people living here on Earth, men and women who could pass for very tall Scandinavians. These were not just Venusians, but people from numerous populated planets or planetary satellites in this solar system. One Martian allegedly said the following to Adamski:

> We live and work here… We have lived on your planet now for several years. At first we did have a slight accent. But that has been overcome and, as you can see, we are unrecognized as other than Earth men.
>
> At our work and in our leisure we mingle with people here on Earth, never betraying the secret that we are inhabitants of other worlds. That would be dangerous, as you well know. We understand you people better than most of you know yourselves and can plainly see the reasons for many of the unhappy conditions that surround you.

When I looked into Adamski back at Naval Intelligence in the Twin Towers, I was able to pull the file that the FBI apparently had put together about him. It included testimony from individuals who claimed that the "Professor" had told them that the United States of America was comparable to the Roman Empire in its last stage of degenerative decline and that seekers of higher wisdom should welcome the impending conquest of its ruins. He had also admitted to these associates that his wartime sympathies had been with Nazi Germany. One wonders whether Adamski did actually travel to Tibet, and whether he perhaps met men from the SS *Ahenenerbe* that Himmler had sent there around the same time to investigate Tibetan esoteric knowledge about the lost world empire of the Aryan race. The file made much of Adamski's connection to "George Hunt Williamson," or as Thompson unmasked him, Michel d'Obrenovic.

Like Adamski, D'Obrenovic was of Eastern European ancestry—*and what an ancestry!* It turned out that the guy was a direct descendant of Prince Lazar I who ruled Serbia from 1371 to 1389. More immediately, he was the grandson of H.R.H. Prince Wilhelm Maximilian Obrenovic Obelitz von Lazar of Serbia. This prince, being the sole survivor of an insurrection in which his royal family was eradicated, was taken in by Antoine I, the King of Saxony, and thereby entered Germanic aristocracy.

In his youth, D'Obrenovic had joined an American Fascist group founded by William Dudley Pelley (1890–1965). After a Near Death Experience in 1928, Pelley became an evangelist for an esoteric form of Fascism. He named his group the Silver Legion and they were informally known as the Silver Shirts, on account of the silver-colored shirts that they wore as a play on Mussolini's Black Shirts. Pelley was able to establish branches of the Legion in almost every American state. The most significant of all of these places, the headquarters of the movement, was set up on a Western ranch near Los Angeles donated by a wealthy heiress — a ranch which, not incidentally, would be reclaimed by Charles Manson and his "family" in the 1960s.

In 1936, Pelley stood as a third party candidate in the race for President of the United States. His open support for Adolf Hitler and the Nazi Party throughout the 1930s became such a bane to the Administration of FDR that he was summoned before the House Un-American Activities Committee in 1940, who ordered federal marshals to shut down every branch of his organization across the country. Despite receiving this stern reprimand, Pelley continued to attack FDR and to oppose war with Germany until he was charged with sedition and high treason in April of 1942. The sedition charge was dropped, but Pelley was convicted and sentenced to 15 years of imprisonment on other charges. Prior to his arrest, Pelley's portrait had appeared on "Wanted" posters throughout the United States.

It is during his imprisonment that Pelley wrote *Star Guests*, which was published in 1950 and laid out his religious philosophy of "Soulcraft." In this opus, Pelley claimed that truly human beings journeyed to Earth from outer space in vast geological antiquity. Darwinian evolution is rejected in favor of an interpretation of the Biblical story of the fallen angels wherein, according to Pelley, the "sons of Heaven" that interbred with mortal women were those members of a cosmic white race who basically committed bestiality by spawning offspring with subhuman apes to produce the various inferior races of the Earth. Pelley was paroled in 1952, the year that Adamski had his second major contact experience, on November 20th, which became the basis for *Inside the Spaceships*. Before joining Adamski's inner circle, as a witness to his earliest contactee experiences, D'Obrenovic was the editor for Pelley's Silver Legion magazine, *Valor*.

It turned out that Thompson's contact information for Williamson — I mean D'Obrenovic — was a bit outdated. *Faustian Futurism* had been forwarded to him, but by the time I arrived in California to meet the man he was living in Los Angeles, not in Santa Barbara. It appeared that he was already having marital difficulties with Holt, and as I gathered from my time with him he had a mistress who was a psychic working with the Los Angeles police department. When he had me meet him at the really swank Biltmore hotel on Grand, I was not offended that he hadn't invited me to his home. Rather, I assumed that he was staying there with his mistress. She didn't join us, though.

He was waiting for me in the somewhat baroquely ornate Renaissance-style Gallery Bar and Cognac Room. Whereas Adamski had died in the mid sixties, D'Obrenovic was, at this time, still only 49 years old. He looked even younger. There was something about him that reminded me of a cunning bandit, despite the fact that he was dressed in a suit. I could easily imagine him hunting ancient mysteries in the Andes, and maybe keeping his eye out for hidden treasure that he could pocket along the way. He had the manuscript of *Faustian Futurism* with him, and although Thompson had probably told him my real name, he addressed me as "Nick" or as "Griffin." He had the air of a man who is not easily impressed, trying to conceal how impressed he was.

"You've somehow perfectly reconstructed the rationale of our project," he said. "Although I would call it Archeo-Futurism, rather than just Futurism. But *Faustian Futurism* has a nice ring to it as a title — and I suppose the Faustian element suggests the cultural-historical dimension of the project, although you could have gone for something more archaic and primordial. Perhaps, *Promethean Futurism*. Doesn't roll off the tongue as melodiously, but it would have been more apt. Maybe just, *Prometheism*." This remark steered us into a conversation about Pilsudski, who had already used that term, and from there into a discussion of the Intermarium project and our common Southeastern European ancestral roots in countries that had fallen within the Soviet Eastern bloc. I took the opportunity to turn toward a discussion of his involvement with Adamski, who I pointed out was also from the same besieged easternmost frontier of the Faustian West.

D'Obrenovic motioned for the bartender to bring us a second round of drinks. Then he explained that Adamski was someone who wound up believing his own propaganda, or rather, the propaganda that he was selected to disseminate. He confirmed for me that Adamski was a military-intelligence operative, which he knew better than anyone else because his purpose in that Contactee circle was to be Adamski's handler. "The writings of someone involved in PsyOps always contain some of the hidden truth. It's intrinsic to disinformation that there's quite a bit of authentic information in it, which is revealed together with falsities rather than simply being hidden." I nodded affirmatively, before going on to complete his thought.

"The rationale is that pure concealment may not be effective *especially in the case of what's behind UFOs,*" I said, eager to convey to him how clearly I understood what he was telling me, "so the perception of what people might glimpse is distorted by providing some background information that is true as context for it, while at the same time mixing this information with lies." Then, as a rejoinder to this D'Obrenovic concluded, "Lies that are often of a preposterous or absurd nature, which are intended to discredit this embedded information in advance of any potential, accidental leakage of it into the public domain."

This had been the kind of operation that Adamski was supposed to carry out, but being a cult leader got to his head. His background in Tibetan mysticism rendered him prone to getting lost in delusions and thought forms projected from his own subconscious mind. He probably really believed that he had been given a tour of a giant mothership orbiting the Earth, when in fact Adamski had only been allowed inside small flying saucers on a couple of occasions and had certainly never left the Earth's atmosphere in them. It was once Adamski suffered this psychological breakdown that "Williamson" broke away from Adamski to salvage the Contactee project under his own direction.

"Where are you staying?" D'Obrenovic asked. "At the Cecil Hotel," I answered. He winced with disgust and looked at me like I had brain damage. "*You know* that place is *haunted* right?! Do you have *any idea* how many people have been raped, mugged, and murdered in that hotel?" After a moment's silence, with somewhat downcast eyes and a slight shrug to accompany my smirk, I said, "I guess I tend to go looking for trouble."

"Well, there's someone I want you to meet, and I'm not asking her to visit you at that godforsaken place. Although, come to think of it, she'd probably be into that." I looked at D'Obrenovic questioningly, and somewhat intrigued. "I'll book you a room here at the Biltmore. That way, we can also spend some more time together. Go check out of the Cecil and collect your suitcase. By the time you get back, I'll have a room prepared for you." It was an offer that, out of sheer curiosity, I wasn't going to refuse.

A few hours later, in the early evening, I had settled into what was an embarrassingly luxurious room at the Biltmore. The room featured antique gilded armchairs, the bathtub was made of solid marble, and every sheet and pillowcase on the canopy bed felt like it was woven from the finest silk. Granted that after I was adopted by my aunt I had been raised in quite a comfortable environment, but this opulence was really over the top and made me slightly uncomfortable—especially since someone else, who I had barely just met, was paying for it. I hated being in anyone's debt.

After shaving for the second time in the day, and changing into the most elegant clothes that I had brought with me (including a vest and silk tie), I went down to the "Music Room" where D'Obrenovic had asked me to rendezvous with him and the mysterious woman who I was supposed to meet. They were sitting at a table near the fountain, under one of the venetian glass chandeliers suspended from the awe-inspiringly ornate ceiling with a fin de siècle wrought-iron skylight as its centerpiece.

The woman had hardly extended her hand when chills ran through my spine and my hair stood on end just looking at her. To begin with, her height put me ill at ease. I don't want to sound like a chauvinist, but having to look up into the eyes of a woman who is a foot taller than you is disconcerting—especially when you are used to being one of the taller people in any group. I was 5'10 and this woman must have been at least 6'9. On that account alone, she attracted quite a bit of attention when she stood up. A number of men sitting at other tables turned their heads to gawk, much to the chagrin of their wives. She had a freakishly high forehead, to the point where it was almost uncanny enough to mar otherwise beautiful features that were as chiseled as a classical sculpture. Her hair was sandy blonde and she had a deep tan, as if she'd spent a lot of her time here in the sun. What was most unsettling were her eyes. They were more deeply set above her prominent cheekbones than is normal, and they were piercingly blue-green — almost the color of turquoise waters in the Mediterranean. You had to see them to believe that someone could actually have eyes that color. But it wasn't the color of her eyes that gave me shivers. It was the look in them, or rather, the way that they were able to look *into me*. Those were the most soul-piercing, and at the same time mesmerizing eyes that I've ever looked into in my life. Even as someone who is used to staring people straight in the eyes, it was hard for me not to look away. It was as if she made me naked before her with that gaze, and at the same time as seeing right through me, offered some kind of entrancing sense of acceptance that was even more disarming.

She didn't let D'Obrenovic introduce her, and now that I think about it, that rogue who had seemed so sharp at the bar earlier today looked like a sheepish lapdog next to this lady. "Pleasure to meet you, Nikolaus. You may call me, Cybele." I bowed and kissed her hand, which was jarringly masculine in its size and strength. She could tell that a shudder ran through my spine when I did, even if she couldn't see the hairs standing up on the back of my neck. Fortunately, we sat down right away, because that wasn't the only involuntary physiological response that I had. I felt my face flushed, and hurriedly drank some of the ice water in my glass. "Do you stay here often," I asked, nervously.

"I find this hotel charming, partly because it is haunted," she said, "Paramhansa Yogananda dropped dead in this very room, you know." I looked at D'Obrenovic with a mixture of annoyance and astonishment. Not because I minded staying at a haunted hotel, but because he had said that I needed to get out of the Cecil since *it* was haunted. He knew just what I was thinking and quick-wittedly came back with, "the difference is that we only have high class ghosts here." "Or in his case, high caste," she added. So she had a sense of humor. "He was an extraordinary man to have known, truly marvelous." I was taken aback by this. As best as I could recall, Yogananda died here in 1952, the same year as Adamski's second most significant encounter. This woman did not look more than — well, come to think of it there was something ageless about her — but, on the face of it, one might take her to be 30 years old at most. She read my mind, and was amused.

"Your proposal is quite revolutionary." I was surprised by this statement. "You've read my manuscript?!" With a wicked smile on her face, and her eyes locked onto me with an implacable stare, she replied, "*He* read it, and I read him. Isn't that right, my dear George?" D'Obrenovic played with the Caesar salad that we had just been served in such a manner as to avoid eye contact. I heard him crunch a crouton with his fork, then another. "I wonder if you realize what you're demanding of people, Nicolaus." She did it again, calling me by the ancient Greek or Roman form of my name. "What would you say to those — and I *assure* you that they have a *clear majority* among my people — who believe that it would be more compassionate to simply de-industrialize the planet, reestablishing more traditional types of societies that are not in any imminent danger of catastrophic misuses of the technologies and techniques that, at this rate, will be openly and ubiquitously developed by no later than the middle of the next century?"

It was now clear to me, without any shadow of a doubt, just who I was dealing with and what the stakes were. She read my mind, again, and cautioned me. "Don't overestimate my importance or influence." She smiled, "I'm what you might call a Public Relations Liaison. That's all. Someone who has a unique perspective, with one foot in this world, where I was mostly raised, and the other foot... well... you know." Still staggered by the implications, and wanting to diffuse the tension before launching into defending a doctrine that I had only contrived to gain access to people who could help me make sense out of my own life, I endeavored to change the subject for a moment. "So, you were raised *here*?" She gave me the breathing room that I needed. "Not *here*, exactly. Colorado. We have extensive property in the Rockies. *We even* pay taxes," she said with a certain jovial cynicism as she raised an eyebrow and twirled her fork. "Ski much?" I asked, trying to be clever. "I'm an expert," she retorted as she attacked the steak that had just been placed in front of us (she had ordered hers rare).

Throughout dinner, the two of us were in deep discussion about the vision of *Faustian Futurism*. It was an odd discussion, because I often didn't need to complete my thoughts out loud or even finish all of my sentences. Her rejoinders to the things that I would say implied her having raced five steps ahead and processed all of the implications of a line of thought that I was just embarking on with one or another statement. Having once been intensely telepathic myself, and still retaining a measure of this ability on account of exercising it in the psychic espionage program at the World Trade Center, I was also able to read some of her thoughts and emotions.

So it was not as surprising to me as it ought to have been when, after we were through with dinner, D'Obrenovic, who had said very little this whole time, got up and almost disdainfully threw his white napkin back on the table before bidding us goodnight. "Don't mind him," she said. "His mistress is upstairs and will make him all better." I looked at her wondering why the mistress hadn't joined us for dinner. "She's a psychic, like you. We didn't want her getting inside your mind — or mine, for that matter. She's not a part of the project."

We lingered only long enough to let D'Obrenovic head up before us, and then, without any need for words to be exchanged about it, we got up from the table and "Cybele", or whatever her name really was, followed me into the elevator and did not press any button other than the one I had pressed for my floor. The hairs were standing up on the back of my neck again. I let her feel that I felt that. She took one of those strong hands and put it on the back of my head, at which point I felt something like a rush of cool air in my crown chakra, followed by a warm sensation slowly filling the rest of my body with an especially intense heat building up along the length of my spine. I walked off the elevator and down the hallway in an almost trance like state, and by the time she followed me into my room, I was extremely aroused. Our rapport was magnetic.

As I looked into her eyes while she removed her dress, I saw that all of the disarming pleasantries she brought to bear at the table had slipped away like a velvet veil. Those were the eyes, and that was the expression, of a ferociously intelligent predatory animal — not a human being as we understand what it means to be "human." She stood there before me brazenly, stark naked. I knew that if I didn't take my clothes off at once, she would tear them off my body with such force that she might also tear through my skin. Once I disrobed, with both of our clothes strewn on the carpet, she literally tackled me. So much for the satin sheets. As I lay there on the floor, I felt as if a panther had mounted me. I tried to hold her waist, but she pinned my arms back with an iron grip as she ground down on my cock. I was relieved at how wet she was, and I psychologically surrendered to being taken by a woman far more powerful than myself. Fortunately, there was something contagious about her magnetic energy that electrified my own body and made me harder, for longer, than I had ever been before. When she came, she let out a cry so primal that it lacerated my heart and reverberated in my blood.

I was still rock hard when Cybele got up off of me, with a wickedly playful look on her face. Her expression had changed to that of a terribly mischievous child. "You wanna go back down and have some desert?!" she asked. "Where I come from, we never get to have desert." I looked down at how stiff I still was, with my body spellbound by her preternatural magnetism. "Is that *stuck*?" she said as she chuckled tauntingly. I was astonished at the rudeness of her manner of expression now, as compared to the way she carried herself at dinner. Actually, it was really refreshing and got me even more excited. I was standing at the side of the bed, and she pushed me down onto it. Finally, the satin sheets and pillows. "Let's fix that, so we can go back down together."

She lunged into the huge bed with me, and rolled my body on top of her perfectly sculpted form. "Fuck me however you like, and fill me." Astonishing. I did as she asked. Although, judging by her attitude, I was not expecting her to have another orgasm, she got inside my head such that she could experience herself through my body in a way that I could tell really aroused her again. So, when I let go into her full bush, which was the same sandy blond color as her hair, with her hands gripping my head and her turquoise eyes piercing mine, she came hard — as if she was coming through me and into herself. Then we sloppily slipped our clothes on and, with unkempt hair, went downstairs to have that desert that she was so childishly insistent on getting, together with another round of drinks. She told me that among her "people" this kind of behavior (indulging in the decadent desert and hard drinking, not the primal sex) was considered degenerate. It was one of the perks of her position that she could bend, or even break, some of their rules.

When we came back upstairs again, this time she brought me to her room — which, if you can believe it, was even more opulent than mine. I noticed a few odd things there as we took our clothes off, but I was too drunk to think much about them before we staggered into bed together. For example, there was something that looked sort of like a briefcase-sized telegraph machine but it was wireless. There was also a pale green glowing phosphorescent sphere about the size of a crystal ball. When we entered the room it was the only light source. She rather hastily covered it with a nearby piece of cloth. At some point, it must have been shortly before dawn, I just barely became conscious enough to notice that Cybele's place in the bed was empty and I wearily fluttered my eyes open to see her sitting in a perfect meditation posture in the middle of the room. Maybe I was dreaming, but I could almost swear that she was glowing blue and floating slightly off the carpeted floor. Then, as I felt something like a cold hand gently brushing against my forehead, I heard her voice in my mind saying "sleep", and so I did.

The next morning, we had breakfast in bed together — another decadent luxury that she seemed to relish indulging in as if it were some abuse of power. Cybele was still naked, having only put on her bathrobe to retrieve our tray when room service brought it to the door. In the morning light I noticed how her tan was totally even across her whole body, with no bikini lines. When she saw me marveling at her, marveling in fact at being in this situation with her, she said, "We're just *people*, you know. *You* remember what it was like to be one of us, don't you?" I did, and I also recalled what had happened to Anna when I remembered being one of *them*. Cybele heard me go through these thoughts, then looked at me somewhat pitifully and said, "I'm sorry." Then, after a moment's silence, she went back to devouring the crispy bacon that she held in her greasy fingers.

D'Obrenovic called her room and arranged things for the day. We met him in the driveway. He was behind the wheel of a stunning retro late 50s black car with tailfins. "Get in," he said to me curtly. I opened the car door for Cybele. These gestures were always rather odd when it came to her, since I knew that I was dealing with a woman who, if she wanted or needed to, could literally tear me apart with her bare hands. I tried to get into the front passenger seat next to D'Obrenovic, but Cybele pulled me into the back seat with her like I was her pet. "I'm glad to see the two *of you* are getting along," he quipped. "Nice car!" When I said this he winced at me in the rearview mirror. "It's *my* car," said Cybele, "I only let him drive it." Wow. George Hunt Williamson, heir to Serbian royalty, Contactee cult leader, and now… chauffeur?! Who *was* this woman?

We drove to the north for about an hour, at which point Cybele gracefully removed the scarf on her neck and tied it around my face to cover my eyes. I knew not to demand an explanation. The car made some erratic turns after that. I could tell we were off the highway and onto some rocky dirt road, and that we were climbing in altitude pretty precipitously. It would have wrecked my nerves if it weren't for the fact that rubbing against Cybele's body had a strangely tranquilizing effect on me. Finally, the car stopped, and she removed the blindfold. D'Obrenovic had already gotten out, and opened the door for us.

As I stepped out behind Cybele, I was awestruck at the breathtaking vista of giant sequoia trees and waterfalls pouring down over steep cliffs, which we beheld from atop the rocky canyon that we were now standing on. I guessed that we were in the San Gabriel Mountains. She took my hand and we followed D'Obrenovic as he led us into a crevice in the rocks that was just barely wide enough to walk through. There was a camouflaged door carved into the rock, with a concealed panel next to it that was revealed by turning a fake outcrop of rock. He typed in an access code and the door slid open. We were met with a rush of cool, damp air and a phosphorescent green glow lit the way ahead as the automatic door slid closed behind us.

Now Cybele took the lead, as D'Obrenovic and I descended rapidly behind her. We were walking fast down broad steps cut into the rock, and illuminated by phosphorescent spheres about the size of a soccer ball embedded into the sheer stone wall to our left side at regular intervals. She led us down to a platform with another door, this one with a shiny metallic surface. After placing her palm on a reader next to the door, it slid open to reveal a decent sized room, maybe about thirty by twenty feet with a fifteen foot tall ceiling. There was another door across the room, on the opposite side as the one through which we had entered. In the room were a row of suits hanging from hooks that came down from the ceiling. Some were black, others pale blue. There were also several glass cylinders large enough to easily accommodate a person.

"Get undressed and go in there," Cybele said to me, as D'Obrenovic, who seemed to already know the routine, was stripping and placing his discarded clothes onto empty hooks that were on the opposite side of the room as the ones with the suits hanging down from them. "After you step inside, hold your arms up, spread your legs apart, and keep your eyes closed until it opens again." I hesitated, partly transfixed once more by the sight of Cybele's nude body as she stepped into one of the cylinders after hanging her dress up. I finally stepped inside one of these devices, which seemed to zap my body with some kind of radiation that I supposed was meant to be decontaminating in nature. Afterwards, I rushed to catch up with the two of them, who were already suited up—Cybele in a pale blue, skintight suit that was made of something like spandex and showed off every curve and crevice of her sculpted body, and D'Obrenovic in a more loose-fitting black suit, also of one piece. "Put the black one on," he told me. There were accompanying boots, which were not as sleek and pointy as the ones Cybele was wearing. Once I was ready, we all went through the other sliding door together, at which point I stopped again to marvel at where I was.

We were on the platform of what appeared to be a vast subterranean monorail station, cut right into the rock. This place was also lit by the phosphorescent spheres, with their eerie pale green glow, but these ones were larger and mounted on the top of stone pillars that tapered upwards. I had hardly been able to take all this in, before a sleek and windowless bullet train slid into the station, magnetically levitating on the rail that led to and from a tubular tunnel bored into the mountain. D'Obrenovic and I followed Cybele onto the train through a curved door that opened upwards like the trunk of a car. Once we were seated in the sterile white, featureless interior of the cabin, this thing *flew* at a speed that I could barely imagine and that was hard to estimate, but in the pit of my stomach I could sense how fast it must have been—despite the fact that there was no turbulence at all. Clearly, this magnetically levitating train had been placed inside a vacuum. There was a barely perceptible pop every now and then, when, I imagined, the air was being sucked out of one section of tunnel after another, each with its own airlock.

At the next station, a man and a woman boarded our compartment. After casting a fleeting glance at us, they seemed to put as much distance between themselves and us as possible. Both were wearing the same pale blue suits as Cybele, except they were not tan and they had platinum blond hair. They also shared the same oddities of her facial features. The man must have been at least 7'5. I got the distinct sense that he saw D'Obrenovic and I as beneath contempt. As for the woman, who occasionally glared at Cybele out of the corners of her eyes, my psychic impression was that she saw Cybele in much the same way as a proper lady would look down on a prostitute. The words "Sister of Mercy" flashed into my mind, at which point Cybele turned her neck and gave me a hard stare before smirking and then staring straight ahead again.

Maybe fifteen minutes had gone by before we reached a station where Cybele got up and motioned for us to follow. She seemed too self-conscious to take my hand in front of the two others, but she did cast a spiteful glance at them on the way out of the train. This station was even larger than the one we had embarked at, and there were other people on the platform. Once we walked through the sliding door, we entered an enormous cavern full of stalactites, some of which were quite frightening because in the phosphorescent light they looked like monstrous creatures. In addition to the dampness that one would expect at this subterranean depth, there was a faint smell of sulfur and cinnamon mixed with the scent of something like cardboard that had been burnt and then gotten wet. I thought I saw some hideous shapes of subhuman stature slinking between distant stalagmites, but when I tried to stare hard at one of them what I saw was an impossibly large owl — so I just put it out of my mind.

As we walked through a roughly hewn tunnel, we came face to face with a man of gigantic stature — maybe 8 or even 9 feet tall — with features like those of the butler from the Adams family. He had to pass close to us, because the tunnel was just barely wide enough for two of these large people to stand side by side within it. As he approached Cybele he muttered something to her in a strange language, and I got the impression that he had no need to say it because she could read his mind and vice versa. But he said it just to make a point, as a gesture of rebuke. Cybele talked back to him defiantly. He stopped and turned around to give D'Obrenovic and I a hard stare, before continuing on his way toward the tube station that we had just come from.

It was a tongue that sounded something like Sanskrit, but softer in the way that Persian is, and with a melodious quality to it, somewhat like Swedish. D'Obrenovic, the linguist and amateur archeologist, could tell what I was thinking, and he said, "these days academics call it Proto-Indo-European." He meant the Aryan root language, but this was no hypothetical reconstruction. They were still speaking it here, fluently, as a living mother tongue. I also noticed that there were inscriptions in this language, written on some of the doors that we walked past as we took several turns through this tunnel network. The script looked like a cross between Mongolian (except oriented horizontally), Tibetan, and hieratic ancient Egyptian. We finally went through one of these doors.

It opened onto a walkway around a vast atrium, lit by a skylight that was presumably providing artificial UV rays because it felt like the sun was pouring in, but we were too far underground for that to be possible. The rocky interior of the cavern had been largely covered by perfect megalithic stonework, with water flowing over it in certain places and covered by verdant shrubbery and vines in other places. (That these would grow here added to my suspicion that the artificial sunlight had UV properties.) At the bottom of the atrium was a plaza or the nexus of a mall, with people converging on it and passing through it from multiple directions. There were geometric sculptures on pedestals, and pools where the water flowing down the stone slabs would collect. The only designs were repetitive geometric patterns, and the only colors were different colored stone. Just a few of the people were wearing the type of skintight bodysuit that Cybele had on. Most wore clothes that looked like something between a robe and a very long jacket, and all of these garments were in drab colors like beige, olive, tan, and ivory.

We took a glass elevator down the side of the atrium to the ground level. Then Cybele led us through the crowd, which wasn't hard considering the fact that these people cleared away from D'Obrenovic and I as if they were Puritans under orders to shun us. We walked at some length down one of the hallways extending out from the plaza, I suppose you could call it a subterranean avenue of sorts. The further we got from the skylight, the more we relied on the illumination of the phosphorescent spheres which were, here as in the tube station, set on pillars like streetlights. In this lane, I stopped dead, startled at the sight of little children playing with one another as they walked down the street with what were presumably their parents. They also stopped when they saw us, and appeared to be intensely curious about D'Obrenovic and I in our black jumpsuits. But their parents grabbed them by the hand and hurried them away from us. Cybele looked at me and smiled, but there was also a profound sadness in her expression and I thought I even saw tears welling up in her eyes.

She led us through a large stone doorframe that looked like polished black granite, and up a series of steps made of what I imagined was a poured stone — like concrete. At the top of the stairs was the interior of an extremely austere apartment, with its own small artificial skylight. There were no decorative flourishes on its cold stone walls and very little furniture. There was, however, a dining table, where a meal had already been laid out — presumably for us — by a downtrodden woman who I could see shuffling things in a back room off to the side, and who gave me the impression that she was a maidservant. Perhaps even, a *slave* — but one incapable of forming any notion of rebellion.

We sat down together at the table. I was quite thirsty by this point, and gulped down the water that Cybele poured for us into metal cups that kept it cool. It tasted like it had minerals in it. I took my cues on how to eat this food from Cybele. Some of it was similar to Mediterranean food, and some to the kind of seafood served in Scandinavia, but other things were quite unfamiliar and I tasted them hesitantly, after watching Cybele eat them. One of these was comparable to honeycomb. We ate in silence, so that the peace and tranquility of this place settled from its stone walls into my bones. Looking back on it, I suppose that this supper was meant to be a kind of communion.

Before we headed back, D'Obrenovic asked to use the restroom and I got the impression that he was doing that just to let me know that there *was* one in case I wanted to go. I followed him, and after he came out he said, "just sit there, it'll do the rest." I was relieved to discover that he was right, since there was no toilet paper in the room. The toilet had some system whereby it would crystalize waste matter before blowing it away as a fine powder and then using jets of water and blasts of hot air to clean you off. It ended with a puff of mild perfume. I was amused by this novelty, which was a welcome relief to the intense emotions that I had felt since entering this subterranean city. I almost had the feeling that, if I stayed here long enough, my life — rather, my lives — on the surface of the Earth would feel like the frantic wanderings of a runaway child are remembered by him once he has been brought back home.

We headed back to the maglev train station, along the same route as we had come. This time there was no one on the train with us, so I asked Cybele, "how far do these tunnels extend?" "On *this* continent? Across the entire United States, both down into Mexico and up into Canada in two directions — toward Alaska, and also toward Greenland, where there are bases for submarine routes that cross the North Atlantic." I looked at her astonished. Then D'Obrenovic broke in, "yeah, we could even take you back home to New York right now — well, close enough to it, if your luggage weren't back at the Biltmore. One of the maglev tunnels connects to an abandoned station in the oldest, deepest levels of Grand Central Terminal. We could be there in less than an hour."

After passing through the changing room again, we emerged from out of the hidden doorway at the top of the canyon to see that it was night. We were far enough to the north of Los Angeles that the stars could be seen pretty clearly, and I took a moment to stare up at them in wonder before getting back into Cybele's black car. This time she didn't stop me from sitting in the front beside D'Obrenovic, and I saw that it was because she wanted to sprawl across the back seat by herself and nap until we got back to LA. The two of us looked back at her in the rearview mirror, and then at each other with an unspoken understanding that could have become the beginning of a real bond.

The overnight concierge was on duty when we returned to the Biltmore, and, since it was a weekday, its opulent hallways were quiet. "I'll take you to the airport tomorrow myself," said D'Obrenovic when bidding us goodnight. My flight from LAX back to JFK was around noon the next day. When we got off on the second floor, I immediately noticed a little girl running down the hallways and playing by herself. It was well after midnight. Cybele registered that I was perplexed and explained, "don't mind her. She's a ghost." Indeed, when we got to the fork in the hallway that she turned down, the girl was nowhere to be seen in either direction. Cybele looked at me like I was being ridiculous as I kept looking down one hallway and then the other. "After *all* you've seen today, *that* perplexes you?" She grabbed my arm and pulled me into the room with her.

As we walked in, she noticed that a message was being typed out on that machine that I glimpsed last night — the one that looked like a wireless telegraphy device. She sat down at the table that it was on, uncovering the small phosphorescent sphere for lighting instead of turning up the room's dimmer switch. I watched her glowing face and fingers as she typed out a reply, walking up to her slowly. She turned slightly toward me in acknowledgement, at which point I dared to place my hands on her shoulders and look over her head down at the machine. I could now see that the letters on its keyboard were in the same script that had been inscribed on the doors in the subterranean city. Another couple of lines came through on the machine, before she got quite annoyed and flipped a switch that shut it off. "They're reprimanding me for having brought you there today." She slipped her arm around my waist, still sitting at the table while I stood next to her. "I wanted to give you a taste of my world – or to remind you, of the world that was once your own. You need to know — you need to re-member — before you threaten to deform what little is left of 'Atlantis' with your *Faustian Futurism*. Not that you *shouldn't* do it!"

Cybele got up and filled the spacious marble bathtub. We threw our clothes onto the bed, and slipped into the water together. It was a strange feeling to be held by her. I guess it should have been the other way around, but I gave into it because at that moment I intuited more clearly than I had thus far, that this woman, despite her youthful appearance and the vulgarity of her occasional, brazenly adolescent manner of expression, was more than old enough to be my mother.

"You know, I have a son" she whispered, after hearing my thoughts. "What's his name?" I asked. "Apollyon," she said. "I don't want him growing up in hiding. He's so creative and could shine in *this* world." Then, with an unexpected tinge of desperation in her voice, she asked, "Can you make us young, again?" When she said that, a series of im-ages flashed through my mind: Friedrich Nietzsche, James Joyce, John Coltrane, Frank Lloyd Wright, Jackson Pollock, Elvis, David Bowie, Jim Morrison, and Jimi Hendrix.

Their science and technology was in some ways far more advanced than ours. There was hardly anything that our physicists, biologists, or engineers would be able to teach them. But when it came to art, literature, and philosophy — they had reached a creative dead end, suffering stasis and stagnation for millennia. "Sing a song to make us young again, Nick. Be a brother to my son."

CHAPTER 7

MASTERING LIGHTNING

y experience with Cybele was so intimate that "close encounter" doesn't come close to doing it justice. Our time together came back to me in vivid detail as I watched the rather sensationalist media coverage of Travis Walton's abduction. On November 5, 1975 a group of seven loggers from Snowflake, Arizona, who were working in the Sitgreaves National Forest witnessed a flying saucer in those woods at the outset of their evening drive back home. It had all of the typical features of close encounters. For example, the object was deathly silent and seemed to just hang in the air. Once it started moving again, it wobbled like a top — as UFOs typically do. One of the men, Travis Walton, got out of the truck that they were all riding in and approached the object, despite the vehement protests and warnings of the other terrified loggers. When Walton got very close, he was struck by a beam of light that lifted him off the ground and then threw him back down hard onto the forest floor. The other men, to their later embarrassment, drove away as fast as possible – leaving Walton for dead. Shortly thereafter, out of a sense of guilt, they drove back but his body was missing. After notifying the authorities, including local Sheriff Marlin Gillespie, a massive search and rescue operation was organized.

Over the course of the next 48 hours, the Navajo County Search and Rescue Team, the Heber Forest Service, and a number of other volunteer groups, canvassed the entire forest, not just on the ground, but also including men using high powered binoculars to search the thinned forest from out of helicopters and private planes. There was no sign of Travis Walton anywhere. The men began to come under suspicion of having murdered their associate and hidden his body. Consequently, they were compelled to submit to polygraph testing. On November 10, Michael Rogers, Steve Pierce, Allen Dalis, Kenneth Peterson, Dwayne Smith, and John Goulette were all hooked up to lie detectors at the Holbrook County Courthouse. The only test that proved inconclusive was that of Allen Dalis, who was known for his hot temper and was being extremely combative and uncooperative, to the point where his polygraph readings were all over the place. As for the others, Cy Gilson, the Arizona Department of Public Safety officer who administered the tests, was grudgingly forced to conclude, "These polygraph examinations prove that these five men did see some object they believe to be a UFO." That statement was all over the news, and it certainly caught my attention.

Still, it was nothing compared to what happened that night at 12:05am, exactly five days and six hours after Travis Walton's abduction. Walton's brother-in-law Grant Neff received a call from an obviously distressed Travis, who had made it to a phone booth at a service station after being deposited on a deserted highway by a flying saucer that he saw shoot straight up into the sky as it departed. Travis thought that only a few hours had gone by. In other words, he had *five days* of what UFO researchers call "missing time." His few hours of memories from the abduction are, however, quite fascinating. Walton remembered these things spontaneously, but was able to process and recount them with less anxiety and stress after undergoing a regression hypnosis performed by Dr. James Harder. This hypnosis was witnessed by a number of other professionals as well, including Dr. Howard Kandell, Dr. Joseph Saults, Dr. Robert Ganelin, Dr. Jean

Rosenbaum, and Dr. Beryl Rosenbaum. They became the first people to hear the astonishing story that the media would widely report, and often misreport, over the coming days and months.

Travis Walton's first memory after being knocked unconscious by the UFO, was waking up on some kind of operating table inside the flying saucer. He was surrounded by short, bulbous headed beings with large almond-shaped eyes and very thin limbs covered by a kind of ivory-colored material that was more like marshmallow than human flesh. After struggling to get free from these beings, an extremely panicked Walton ran through the craft's hallways like a caged animal until he found his way into an empty room with a chair that had buttons on its console and that afforded a view of the stars *through its curved walls that seemed to become transparent* — although he wondered if this was actually a kind of projection, as in a planetarium. Finally, a man came to retrieve Walton, who was very relieved to encounter what appeared to him to be another human being – rather than the monstrous "aliens" that he had dealt with earlier. Upon reflection, Walton realized that these "aliens" may have been very sophisticated android robots.

The man took Walton out of the saucer into what appeared to be a hanger or perhaps a shuttle bay inside of a much larger craft. A number of flying saucers like the one that he had been inside of were parked here. The man then led Walton into another smaller sized room, where he was even more relieved to encounter three other *people* — two men and one woman – all of whom were also blonds. Walton has had an artist carefully render his description of these people, and the paintings produced depict individuals that have a vaguely Nordic look to them. They had sandy blond hair, were tan as if they had been in the sun, and what especially struck Walton was how perfect their features and skin were – with the men having faces as smooth as that of the woman. Her hair was longer than theirs, which was (by our standards) already long for men. They all wore skintight pale blue bodysuits, which revealed their exquisite physiques. None of them would answer any of Walton's questions, and they responded to

him only with a slightly empathetic smile that suggested they were being tolerant. They put him on another table, holding him down gently
after he began to resist, at which point the woman placed something
like a wireless oxygen mask over his face and he became unconscious.
The next thing Travis knew, he was laying on that cold highway
around midnight.

In the late fall of 1975, when the Travis Walton abduction was all
over the news, I started watching a new series called *Space 1999*, which
was also a British production. The first episode of *Space 1999* was titled
"Breakaway" and after watching it, with *The Prisoner* in mind, I began
to formulate the idea of a "Breakaway Civilization." The show depicted
a relatively near future where the Moon had been colonized. I mar-
veled at how no one seemed to realize that the aesthetics in shows like
this, the way that people in the futuristic Moon facilities were dressed,
the architecture of their living and working places, and even their
mannerisms, were all deeply Fascist — albeit in a modernist sense that
represented a kind of extension of Italian Futurism into the space age.

In any case, this opening episode was about how certain "magnetic" anomalies on – or within — the Moon cause it to break away
from Earth's orbit and essentially become a space ship. It occurred to
me that the writers of this show had access to classified information
about the Moon being a hollow, artificial construction that is quite
possibly capable of propulsion — since it was brought from elsewhere
and parked in Earth's orbit to begin with. The "breakaway" seemed
to me to be a metaphor for the breakaway of a futuristic Fascist elite
from the civilizations of Earth and their becoming a space-faring civilization in their own right. At one point, the lead character, played by
Martin Landau, exclaims that "we're sitting on the biggest bomb ever
invented." Given the episode's focus on lethal magnetic "radiation",
which is explicitly contrasted with nuclear radiation, this seemed
to me to be a reference to the magnetic bomb that Adamski's Space
Brothers were worried that we would create if they shared the technology of gravity control with us.

In a subsequent episode, titled "Black Sun", which aired the day after Walton's abduction, the crew of this space ship Moon confronts the danger of a black hole. It could hardly have been lost on the writers that the "Black Sun" was an esoteric Nazi symbol. I suspected that they even knew that it was what Project Chronos was attempting to create, namely an artificial singularity or space-time vortex that could both be tapped for unlimited energy and also serve as an anti-gravity propulsion system.

I thought back to something that Williamson had told me in the course of our final conversation as he drove me to the airport in Los Angeles. "It's about power," he said. "As in Nietzsche, *The Will to Power?*" I had replied somewhat naively. He smirked and said, "Sure. But I mean literally. Power." I looked at him searchingly, "Like electricity?" His eyes lit up. "Yes — and magnetism. Mastering lightning, and wielding magnetic power. Controlling the motor of the world."

I had to disappear. I knew too much, and I wanted out of this nightmare. *Could* I disappear? I would have to figure out how. Meanwhile, I couldn't bare to stay in my aunt's apartment. I still had the elegant wooden dining table that Thompson had sat around in the living room, when I had just been taken in as an orphaned child. I remembered my recurring childhood dream of the old man who lived out of suitcases in hotel rooms, the last of which I had identified as a room in the Hotel New Yorker based on what I recalled of its lobby from those dreams.

One cold day in December of 1975, I had a false identification manufactured at a place in the East Village. Then I packed my suitcases and checked into the New Yorker under an assumed name, paying cash for a stay that I explained I might want to extend — indefinitely. The chandeliers that hung over the lobby were so eerily familiar that they gave me goose bumps. I requested a room with a clear view of the Empire State Building. They said they had a few rooms with that view available, on the 28th, the 30th, and 33rd floors. With my penchant for occult symbolism, I obviously chose the one on the 33rd floor. The clerk gave me a glance that I only understood later. It was room number 3327.

When I walked into the dark room my eyes were immediately drawn to a spectacular view of the Empire State Building, already lit for the nighttime, as a blood orange sunset seared the skyline of downtown Manhattan through one of the windows. I set my suitcases down, and without flipping the light switch, I sat on the bed to take in the vista. The strangest sensation came over me as I sat there in the darkening room and watched the city lights start sparkling against the evening sky. In all my life, I never felt closer to being at home.

I laid down and fell asleep, in my clothes, without ever turning on the light. When I awoke, I was startled to find that the bed had shifted closer to the wall. The room was still dark, but I could tell right away that it was full of strange things. There were locked metal cabinets and filing drawers across from me. The walls were covered with large framed drawings. There was a big wooden crate in the corner of the room. I was severely disoriented. In fact, for a few panicked moments that seemed like an eternity I could not for the life of me remember who I was. My body felt extremely frail as I struggled to get up out of bed. I almost fell onto the floor, before remembering to reach for the cane by the bedside.

Then, I stumbled across the room, leaned on a cabinet, and looked over at one of the drawings. I could barely make it out in the indigo light of the predawn hour that was beginning to come in through the curtains. In a thick dark wooden frame there was a horizontal drawing of a polygonal tower studded with illuminated windows, which tapered toward the top into a sphere that appeared to be radiating luminescent energy into the night's sky. A more low-lying and broader rectangular building was immediately behind the tower. This structure was in the foreground, and it was separated by water from what appeared to be the distant skyline of Manhattan. Beams were emanating from the top of the tallest skyscraper. In the distance between them, sleek airships — a number of them wingless — streaked through the night, with rays extending out from them as if to suggest that, like the city itself, these were being powered wirelessly by the tower.

Before I could even remember who I was, this drawing triggered an associational image in my mind. It was of a tower similar to the one depicted, but out in the secluded countryside and built much more crudely. It was constructed of wooden beams and surmounted with a metallic mesh dome, which was shooting artificial lightning into the night and producing a radiant glow similar to the aurora borealis. The townspeople were terrified of it. No, they were terrified of *me*. Then it started to come back to me.

I looked at another one of the framed posters. There was a man sitting on a chair, as if calmly reading a book, inside a huge room — a veritable Frankenstein's laboratory. He was surrounded by high pillars on tripods. One of these, which was encircled by an iron cage, was topped off by a metallic sphere that was pouring artificial lightning bolts out into the room to be caught by the tall black cylinders. I recognized myself as the master of lightning in that photograph.

There was a blue glow in the room now, and in this dim light I could see that it was full of crates and boxes stamped "N.T." I went over to the window and pulled aside the transparent curtains to see how close it was to dawn. Snow was falling gently in the chasm between my window and the Empire State Building, which had been built on the ruins of the magnificent Astor Hotel, with its Peacock Alley, that I had called home for the best years of my life. They could at least have gone ahead with plans to use the top of the new skyscraper as a dock for airships arriving from Europe. If Morgan hadn't killed my plans to wirelessly power airships rather than filling them with flammable gas, the Hindenburg Zeppelin would never have exploded and spooked Mayor La Guardia into forcing the owners of the Empire State Building to turn their proposed airship port into an "observation deck." There would, at this moment, be wirelessly powered airships gliding through the skies over the kind of Manhattan that Hugh Ferriss had dreamed of.

Instead, after having appropriated my patents, Morgan had secreted away the technology. From various contacts of mine throughout the intervening decades I had learned that his Chase Bank was funding a private group of Prussian industrialists and engineers based in isolated parts of South America, wherefrom they were fielding an already large fleet of airships so fantastical in their design that they would put the imaginings of Jules Verne to shame. From what I was given to understand, the latest models of these craft were also capable of diving into the ocean like submarines. An immaculately dressed and brash young representative of this group even approached me at one point. This was at the bar of the Hotel Astor, my former 'home,' which stood right where the Empire State Building now rose up to crown the skyline. I rejected his offer to join them on account of it being conditional on my "disappearance" from the public world. You see, these men that Morgan was funding, or "supermen" as they saw themselves with their utter contempt for humanity at large, had broken away from society to form their own occulted civilization. When I refused to strop striving to raise up mankind as a whole, they warned that my Promethean hubris would break me. They called themselves the "Atlantis Society" or, in German, *Thule Gesellschaft*.

As I contemplated the snow, I suddenly became deeply depressed at the realization that it was Christmas morning. Maybe that's why my memory had just failed so badly, that memory so extraordinary that, in my youth, I could memorize whole books and, later in life, afforded me the ability to work out any design in my mind without committing the invention to paper until it had been perfected and needed to be sent to the patent office. Maybe I *wanted* to forget why, yet again, I was alone on Christmas, the day of the saint of my namesake, at the age of 87.

The spirit of Christmas, of Saint Nikola, had defined my lifelong endeavor to empower and liberate mankind by dramatically increasing industrial energy, making the worldwide wireless communication of information possible, and laying the groundwork for automatons who would one day free men from all manner of drudgery. This Christmas of 1942, broken, abandoned, and nearly penniless, I was waiting for the world to receive one last gift from me — a weapon that could bring an end to this current war in Europe, stop Fascism, and render futile all future wars.

A small-scale working prototype of the Teleforce device was inside one of the two locked safes in my room, not the smaller green safe — the larger grey one. The press had hyped it up as a "Death Ray" that would burn enemy planes and ships out of the air and sea by hurling precisely directed lightning bolts, like Zeus striking his foes from Olympus by pointing his divine finger. In actuality, it was a particle beam weapon. Particles of a mercury isotope supercharged by electromagnetic rotation inside of a spherical container would be channeled out of a gun in the form of a plasma that could remain a coherent ray over long distances. This ray could wreck any target almost instantaneously.

After the Nazis seized power in Germany, I tried to sell the Teleforce system to the United States. Then, when my adopted country was uninterested, I turned to the British. They also declined. I even tried to sell the designs for an array of seven of these devices to the government of Yugoslavia, to be placed at various strategic locations in my homeland in order to protect it from Nazi invasion. After all, the King visited me here and, embarrassed at my apparent poverty, he volunteered a stipend to support my most basic living expenses, so I thought he might accept the proposal. But the Yugoslav government dismissed old Tesla as a mad scientist suffering from delusional senility.

Finally, increasingly convinced of the danger of Nazi Germany's expansionist ambitions, in 1935 I made contact with representatives of the AMTORG Trading Corporation of the Soviet Union. They drew up a contract for Teleforce that was dated April 20th, not incidentally Hitler's birthday. I was never allowed to sign that contract. Instead, two G-men in black suits barged their way into my room at the New

Yorker and explained to me that they were aware of my dealings with "the Reds." Apparently, they had been monitoring my phone calls from the switchboard at the top of the New Yorker, which was then the largest telephone communications facility in the world. The men, who threatened in no uncertain terms to revoke my citizenship and re-classify me as an "alien," identified themselves as agents of the Office of Strategic Services (OSS). They had been sent by a Dr. Vannevar Bush. It also turned out that Fitzgerald, my associate and assistant, was actually an OSS spy whom they had tasked to pass on to them every piece of scientific and technical information that I shared with him. The two men in black moved into a room on my floor at the hotel, and from then on I essentially resigned myself to living as a prisoner. This was when I started using carrier pigeons to secretly continue my communications with the Soviet agents who had been interested in using Teleforce to defend against Nazi German territorial expansion. The communist spies would wait in Bryant Park for my tagged pigeons to arrive with coded messages.

Despite the risk of slipping on the snow, I went for my habitual walk in Bryant Park that Christmas morning. Between the Hotel New Yorker and the park, I ran across a drunk dressed as Santa Claus, ringing his bell in an attempt to solicit donations to the Salvation Army from every passerby. I've never stopped believing in Santa and his elves. By comparison, Christ and his angels are a cruel joke. Santa runs a smaller but more trustworthy operation. What's hardest for him is to keep up that jolly public face, because the truth is that he's usually thinking of all the good little children that he just didn't have it in his power to help even though he's tried his best. He cries so desperately into that long white beard from out of his whole soul. That big stomach of his is all cotton stuffing, you know. Part of the public image. The truth is that he's cried himself damn near down to a skeleton all the while he works around the clock. St. Nick knows that no one will be left to help him in his old age. All the little elves will be put away in cupboards then, and Winter will only bring a howling wind to dry the children's tears.

When I arrived at the park, I leaned on my cane with both hands for a few moments, marveling at the rainbow colored lights on the brightly lit Christmas tree standing tall against the white marble of the rear façade of the New York Public Library. As I struggled not to fall while opening my bag of breadcrumbs for the pigeons, I was reminded of how Mephistopheles restored Faust to youth and I wondered whether, at this point, I would accept such a devil's bargain if it meant living long enough to ensure that my inventions would save the world from a Fascist victory in the current war.

It was Goethe's *Faust* that, at the zenith of my youth, had inspired me to invent the alternating current. I had been studying at the University of Prague in Bohemia. During a stroll through the city park of Prague with my good friend at that time, who often recited poetry with me on such walks, I was suddenly reminded of a passage from Goethe's masterwork, the entirety of which I had committed to memory. You see, the sun was just setting, and when I beheld the glowing solar disk, these verses from *Faust* came to mind:

> The glow retreats, done is the day of toil;
> It yonder hastes, new fields of life exploring;
> Ah, that no wing can lift me from the soil,
> Upon its track to follow, follow soaring!

> A glorious dream! Though now the glories fade.
> Alas! The wings that lift the mind no aid
> Of wings to lift the body can bequeath me.

Just as soon as I recited these lines to my companion, a flash of light filled my mind of the kind that often preceded my intensely precise visualizations. What was revealed in that flash was the design of a motor powered by alternating current, essentially the same diagram that I would present to the American Institute of Electrical Engineers six years later. At once, I broke a stick off one of the park's trees and drew this wonder wheel in the sand for my friend. Four coils arranged in a cross around a motor's circular frame were alternately activated using electromagnets in order to reverse the direction of an electric current running through the circuit. The whole contraption looked a bit like a solar wheel, or Swastika, which I presume is why the idea happened upon me while contemplating the setting sun.

The prospect of seeing through the industrial manufacture and implementation of the so-called "death ray", albeit for the sake of world peace, would not be my only temptation to accept a Faustian bargain that could restore my youth and vitality. Nor would the other tempting prospects be restricted to the realization of uncompleted or suppressed technological projects, such as the World Wireless system that was buried when my tower at Shoreham on Long Island was dynamited some years after Morgan defunded it. Rather, my greatest regret is not pursuing the romance offered to me by the Divine Sarah.

Of all the women who attempted to seduce me away from my single-minded devotion to technological invention and scientific innovation, Sarah Bernhardt was in a class of her own. It was at one of her parties that I had met Swami Vivekananda, and began conversations on *prânâ* and *akâshâ* that were indispensable to my formulation of an etheric Physics model at odds with that of Einstein. Far from being a mere actress, Sarah was a brilliant woman with a penchant for mystical contemplation and she relished participating in these dialogues.

One of these conversations was particularly memorable. It was my only heated argument with Vivekananda. First of all, don't let anyone tell you that the Swami was a vegetarian — as he sometimes claimed to be. This particular conversation of ours took place in a back room at Delmonico's, my favorite restaurant in New York. Not only did Vivekananda enjoy his steak, he was also quite a connoisseur of whisky — to the point where he sent back an Old Fashioned *at Delmonico's!* Sarah was amused by this. I was not, especially given that I was a regular, so I looked at the waiter rather apologetically.

We were arguing over the socio-political structure of the *varnas* or "caste system" and its relationship to the cosmology of the *Yugas* or "world ages" in Sanatana Dharma. The Swami took the standard view that the castes were a way for souls to practice various forms of Yoga or disciplined devotion appropriate to their level of respective devolution, all the way from the *Bhakti* Yoga of low caste people to the *Jnana* and *Raja* Yoga of the highest caste people, and thereby evolve back toward union with *Brahman* over the course of many successive lifetimes. The color-coding of the caste system, the name of which, *Varna*, literally meant "color", had originated as a way to segregate people of vastly different levels of ability and understanding, so that disembodied souls in the transitional state between one incarnation and the next would not get mixed and be born into the wrong caste. It was, he explained, a means of establishing psychical distance and differentiation, so that people could be born into conditions that resonate with their own spiritual state and are most suitable for the further development of their *atman*.

Vivekananda knew that I was no egalitarian, but he was somewhat taken aback at the vehemence with which I attacked Hindu theology for the integral role that the caste system plays in any authentic version of it. I pursued three lines of argument against this system. Firstly, it conceived of human beings as *types* rather than as individuals and thereby reaffirmed unreflective collectivism. Secondly, given that human beings are in fact individuals, at least to one or another degree, in any actual caste society it is quite possible and even likely that certain brilliant individuals will wind up being born into the wrong caste and consequently be subjected to treatment that is detrimental to their spiritual development and that deprives them of an opportunity to benefit others. Thirdly, this entire caste hierarchy, I argued, is stratified upwards in the direction of the *daevas* — so that not only are the *Kshatriyas* or knightly warrior caste reduced to servants of the *Brahmins* (which in itself I did not find all that objectionable, since it subjugates military power to spiritual refinement) but the *Brahmins* themselves are turned into mere servants of, or attendants to, the *daevas*.

If one were to mistakenly believe that the "gods" are only mythical beings and objects of superstitious faith, that would be one thing. There would still be a question about the content of these myths and how the *Brahmins* were using them to control this caste society. However, once one recognizes that the *daevas* are really existing beings — as real as you and I — *and that they are often manipulative, deceptive, power-hungry, and even tyrannically sadistic* then the entire caste system has to be called into question from the top down. By the time we had this conversation, *Gospel of the Buddha* had become one of my favorite books and so I reminded Vivekananda that this rejection of the *daevas* as paragons of enlightenment, and even a recognition that there is more opportunity for enlightenment in the human realm than on the planets of these *daevas* deluded by their luxury and power, had been one of the Buddha's key insights.

Closely connected to my rejection of the caste system was an equally impassioned opposition to the *Yuga* cosmology, which unfortunately, even the Buddhists seem to have unthinkingly adopted from the Hindus. By the time I launched into this, the Swami's eyes were bugging out and he was looking around nervously for the waiter so that he could order himself another scotch on the rocks. Sarah was looking at me with the kind of admiration that one has for some predatory beast, like a Bengal tiger. She knew that Vivekananda, who was now being schooled, was used to being treated like a guru.

I told him that I thought the Hindu conception of world ages was regressive. I believe that I even characterized it as "retarded." Two main problems were the focus of my critique of this conception. The first was that a view of declining world ages, with each epoch more degenerate than the one preceding it, leading up — or rather, down — to the present *Kali Yuga* or "Dark Age" (associated with the goddess Kali) is profoundly inimical to fostering human progress. My entire life's work was to power the engine of progress on this planet, with all of my scientific research and technological inventions being merely a means to transform human society, on a planetary scale, in a utopian direction. Ever since I arrived as an immigrant here I had accepted the motto of New York, *Excelsior* or "Ever Upwards", as my personal mantra, one reflected in this city's skyscrapers, such as the Woolworth Building, where I was proud to have had an office. Then, there was a second, related problem. When contemplated within the context of cosmic eternity, any cyclical view of time ultimately implicates a repetition of all events — not necessarily after only one complete cycle, but ultimately. Cyclical time denies the possibility of infinite creativity in the same way as that thought experiment of Nietzsche's which I always found so contradictory to the rest of his Promethean ideas, namely "the Eternal Return of the Same."

These problems with the *Yuga* cosmology were inextricable from my objections to the *Varna* system insofar as putatively "proper" social organization in terms of the castes is supposed to decline together with the world ages, such that in the Kali Yuga many of those who ought to be Brahmins and Kshatriyas fall through the cracks and are crushed at the bottom of a debased materialistic society dominated by merchants, thieves, and thugs. I granted to Vivekananda, that it is certainly the case that in a world dominated by industrialists and financiers — such as Morgan, and his associate Rockefeller — many undeserving and avaricious people who are ruthlessly driven by the basest passions thrive while certain brilliant individuals have their light snuffed out to the detriment of humanity. Had this conversation taken place later in my life, especially now on this cold Christmas day, so many years after being defunded by Morgan and reduced to humiliating destitution, I would have conceded this even more readily. Nevertheless, I argued — and would still maintain — that a caste system will never function as a true meritocracy that rewards the most visionary and creative individuals. This is precisely because creativity, when seen through the lens of the *Yuga* cosmology, can only appear to be subversive deviance.

We are not living in the most decadent and degenerate age of the world. Rather, we are fortunate to live in the epoch of the greatest degree of creativity and innovation known to human history. Even Atlantis, I argued, was no evidence against this. I explained to Vivekananda that the bygone antediluvian world empire had collapsed precisely because, despite possessing certain types of relatively advanced technology, it was locked within a caste system — actually within the very socio-political order that was the model for the Hindu *Varna* conception. On the whole, the people of Atlantis were not somewhat more enlightened denizens of a world age less degenerate than our own, namely that of the *Treta Yuga*. Rather, they were almost subhuman in their relative unconsciousness as compared to the modern individual — let alone geniuses of our time.

I concluded by saying that it all came down to a faith in energy. The Hindu socio-political and cosmological conceptions were radically conservative in the literal sense. Their felt need for conservation came from a lack of faith in infinite energy, or unlimited potential. Here, Sarah closed the conversation by adding, "Life engenders life. Energy creates energy. It is by spending oneself that one becomes rich." I smiled, and got the check.

Certainly, I was being hounded by wealthier and more influential socialites than Sarah. These were women who could have secured funding for my projects, but who also would have wanted to cage me in the domestic life of a dutiful husband. That was out of the question. Sarah was nothing like that. She was not looking for a husband, nor could I have expected fidelity even if I had agreed to become a longterm lover of hers.

She had many lovers, some of whom she brought along on her travels bound into coffins. Her practice was to die to herself in a coffin and reemerge from it as the tragic character she was contracted to play on the stage. When she was not using a coffin for this purpose, it sometimes became a suitcase to carry one or another man who had fallen under her spell. It was probably also her ironic way of suggesting that, after a while, such men became baggage.

Sarah loved me, because I was nothing like them. She confessed that I was the first man that she could really be friends with. What she proposed, on so many visits to my old laboratory, was an intimate friendship, one without boundaries, and which would never become binding. My old pal Sam Clemens, better known by his penname "Mark Twain", had met Sarah on a couple of occasions, and thought I was crazy for not taking her up on it.

The truth is that my various complexes, including an aversion to women's jewelry and an antipathy to touching hair, were crippling obstacles in the way of any attempt to develop this kind of intimate rapport. I would be lying if I said that it was simply my single-minded determination not to be distracted from my work. One time, when I met her at Penn Station, I was struck dumb by the sight of her without any jewelry and with her dark wavy hair tightly bound by a crimson turban. I was flattered to the point of embarrassment that she had done this in an effort to get closer to me. This was one occasion when instead of taking her to my laboratory at 8 West 40th Street, I brought Sarah back to the Astor Hotel where I lived.

Oh the warmth of the steam that rose from the hot bath that she took in my room, wearing only the crimson turban, and the cold of the snow crunching beneath my beat up shoes now! The unpretentious frankness and searing honesty of how she expressed her erotic attraction to me that night, her ardent but patient desire to know her enigmatic friend better, was the most polished mirror that anyone has ever held up to my own inadequacy and limitations.

If I could change one thing in my overly long life, it would be to have had a more ecstatically open and enduring relationship with Sarah. Now, to the great annoyance of the maid and other hotel staff, my closest female companion was one of my two carrier pigeons — the one that the manager had briefly seized when she got disoriented and crash landed onto another floor of the New Yorker. But then I thought of what Faust says to Helen of Troy in Part II of Goethe's magnum opus: "The mind looks neither back nor beyond. This present time alone, Helen, is purest bliss." I would no more have meant this, had I ever been able to say it to Sarah, than Faust means it when he says it to Helen, who is supposed to be the embodiment of Beauty.

I became so absorbed in the old man's reminiscences that, when I awoke again in his deathbed the next morning, I had total recall not only of this lucid dream reliving his lonely last days, but of many experiences from earlier in his life. The disjointed images of my recurring dreams in childhood now fit into a deeper and much broader context. It was so uncanny walking out into Bryant Park that morning, and standing where he — I mean where I — had stood toward the end of my dream, seeing how things had changed since then and how much had stayed the same. The darkly magnificent Radiator Building towered over the park in the same menacingly Gothic way that it had then. Only its gilded details had faded, having been caked in soot.

One thing was certainly different. On the way into the park, on the corner of West 40th street, I looked up at the yellow street sign that said "Nikola Tesla Corner." This corner had been chosen, not because of its proximity to the New Yorker, but because one of the last offices that I could afford to have was at 8 West 40th Street. I walked over to the New York Public Library and spent the day there reading *My Inventions and Other Writings*. What had not come back to me spontaneously, flooded into my mind as I sat there absorbed in the pages of a relatively slim autobiography written by Tesla around the age of 60. By the time I finished, they were getting ready to close the main reading room for the night. On my way out, I looked with changed eyes at the lights of the Empire State Building through the semi-circular windows cut into the high ceilings. It was almost as if I was giving *him* the eyes of a time traveler. Tesla, the ardent Eugenicist, would have been terribly disappointed by this most un-Faustian future.

After I went to bed back at the New Yorker, I had a horrific nightmare. My withered and emaciated corpse — I mean, Tesla's dead body — was lying there beneath me. I was hovering toward the ceiling and looking down on it, as a whole group of men in black suits moved rapidly around the room, opening crates and boxes, and sifting through papers. It seemed to me that it was the middle of the night on the day after I had died. They moved a whole bunch of the crates and boxes down the hallway to the room that they had, for years now, occupied on my floor. They also took the safe with the Teleforce device in it, which three of the men struggled together to move. That backstabbing bastard, Fitzgerald, was with them and he kept saying something to the other men about how the materials that were left in my room, the ones that they didn't "need to bother with" were going to go to someone named "Trump." But what really made this a nightmare is that the whole group of these men were directed by *a woman*. It was my aunt, Nikita.

Moreover, as I stared down at her, partly through Tesla's disembodied eyes, and partly with my own consciousness and memories as Nikolai, I realized that this putatively "Russian" woman was the ringleader of the supposed "Soviet" agents who had presented themselves as negotiators on behalf of the AMTORG Trading Corporation. No wonder they had chosen Hitler's birthday to date their fake contract! These people were not communist spies – they were *Nazi spies* who had entrapped me into a supposedly "Un-American" act of "communist collaboration" so that they could imprison me here. The OSS agents who had been assigned as my wardens at the New Yorker were *double agents*, American Fascists aligned with the Third Reich from within the US Government. Who knows how long they had been spying on me and whether they had interfered to make sure that my offer of Teleforce to the US Department of the Navy was not accepted, because *they didn't want America* to be able to use this "Death Ray" to defend against a Nazi aerial invasion or naval armada from across the Atlantic.

After the men cleared out of my room, and Fitzgerald left with them, making sure to replace the "Do Not Disturb" sign that would prevent the hotel staff from discovering my body for another day or two, Nikita stayed behind with my dead body. I watched as she stripped stark naked, draping her clothes over the chair at my desk, before getting into the bed with my already rotting corpse. She held my head—I mean, Tesla's skull—running the fingers of one hand through his hair and those of the other, backhandedly, down his gaunt cheek. "Come to me, Nikolai," she whispered. "Be mine." I felt like a boa constrictor was tightening its grip on my soul—then I woke up, drenched in sweat.

CHAPTER 8

WONDER WHEEL

It took about a week's stay at the Hotel New Yorker for me to clear everything that I planned to take with me out of the apartment at 77th and Cherokee that had been my home since I was orphaned. It was another month before I was able to get rid of it on the real estate market, thereby replenishing the small fortune in my bank account before it had been much depleted by my living expenses.

If I had really been wise about choosing where to disappear to, I would not have moved to Coney Island. Nostalgia has always been an Achilles' heel for me. Not only did I grow up down the shore, at Brighton Beach, Anna also drowned herself there. Besides, the neighborhood was becoming so decrepit, crime infested, and rife with gang violence that no one would think to look for me in this godforsaken ghetto, let alone in a low-income housing project. I had rented a two bedroom unit under a false name, and with the offer of a deposit large enough that it could not be refused. By the end of the five years that I would live there, the second half of the 1970s, Coney Island would become nothing less than a post-apocalyptic wasteland, almost as bad as the South Bronx. In some ways, worse.

The rundown, beachfront amusement park certainly contributed to the perversity of the place. Unlike the South Bronx, which had become a racially homogenous black ghetto, where one knew exactly what to expect, Coney Island was still pretending to be a place for working class white families to come for "fun in the sun." That made it much more twisted than the South Bronx or certain similarly devastated and crime ridden neighborhoods in Harlem and Brooklyn. Then there were the Brighton Beach Russians, just one neighborhood over, who often strolled to Coney along the coastline. They were their own kind of gangsters, much more ruthless than the Russians I remembered from my childhood there.

I confess that the amusement park was also one of the most alluring aspects of the locale for me. Without its being there, an odyssey to the place of my childhood and of my beloved's suicide would not have sufficed to seduce me into self-exile here. The cheap thrills, freakish curiosities, and lurid colored lights all conspired to turn the Wonder Wheel into a metaphor for the absurdity, not just of *this* life, but of *any* and *every existence* bound to the wheel of rebirth, without any edifying law of karma.

As if Coney Island wasn't dangerous enough during the day, within short order of having moved there, I became a creature of the night. My "days" generally began in the early afternoon. Over the course of several cups of coffee, the first of which was accompanied by eggs to soak up the previous night's liquor, I did a couple of hours research reading and several hours of writing each day. Then, in the late afternoons, I would take a stroll along the boardwalk, smoking one cigarette after another. I was becoming a chain smoker. There was a bar there named "Atlantis" that I liked to stop at for drinks, despite the rough clientele. I never ceased to appreciate it as a commentary on how much like a simulacrum this entire, decaying modern world appeared to be when viewed against the backdrop of the Neptunian realm beneath the waves that I had been tasked to spy on. The whole of it appeared to be a reflection in a funhouse mirror.

In the early evening, during or just after sunset (depending on the season), I would listen to my favorite records. These included *In the*

Court of the Crimson King, the debut album of King Crimson, *Agents of Fortune* by the Blue Oyster Cult, Pink Floyd's *Dark Side of the Moon,* and numerous albums of The Doors. My favorite song, from out of all of these albums, was "Epitaph" by King Crimson:

> The wall on which the prophets wrote
> Is cracking at the seams
> Upon the instruments of death
> The sunlight brightly gleams
> When every man is torn apart
> With nightmares and with dreams
> Will no one lay the laurel wreath
> When silence drowns the screams
>
> Confusion will be my epitaph
> As I crawl a cracked and broken path
> If we make it, we can all sit back and laugh
> But I fear, tomorrow, I'll be crying
> Yes, I fear, tomorrow, I'll be crying
> Yes, I fear, tomorrow, I'll be crying
>
> Between the iron gates of fate
> The seeds of time were sown
> And watered by the deeds of those
> Who know and who are known
> Knowledge is a deadly friend
> If no one sets the rules
> The fate of all mankind, I see
> Is in the hands of fools

By that time in my life, at the not-so-tender age of 28, every line of this song spoke to me. I listened to its lyrics religiously.

At night I would get on the subway at Stillwell Avenue and disembark in Greenwich Village. I had so little contact with fellow students and faculty at the New School that the chance anyone would recognize me as a fugitive PhD student was slim to none. Obviously, what I was more concerned about was being apprehended as a fugitive

Naval Intelligence operative. But I doubted very much that Hal would frequent the restaurants and nightclubs that became my refuge. My favorite of these was a certain *Darvish*, which served Persian food and featured live bands playing both Western and Persian popular music for the clientele on their dance floor. They were especially fond of disco, including some fairly impressive disco music that was apparently being made in Iran.

I had been following the Shah of Iran closely, for obvious reasons. If I ever saw him on television, I would stop to listen carefully. By the year's end of 1975, I was extremely disturbed by two things — although I suppose I ought to have been relieved by them. First, the Shah had not publicly tested nuclear weapons in the way that I had envisioned during my off-the-record remote viewing sessions at Stanford, the ones that had supposedly proven me worthy of recruitment by Naval Intelligence. Second, Richard Nixon had been forced to resign the Presidency on the brink of impeachment over the Watergate scandal.

These two events seemed connected to me. I could not help but to wonder who those men were that convinced Nixon, about a year after my remote viewing session, to trust them to break into the Democratic National Committee headquarters in the Watergate building. I suspected that they were CIA agents, and that their purpose was to remove Nixon from office before he could encourage the Shah to turn Iran into a military nuclear power. If that was where the changes to history ended, one might be forgiven for imagining that I had given way to paranoia. Subsequent events in Iran, at the very close of the decade would, however, confirm that I had in fact changed the course of events. But let me not get ahead of myself.

Sometimes instead of spending most of the night at Darvish or some other club, I would go to see films at a couple of the more artistically-inclined cinemas in the village. The two that made the deepest impression on me, and which I went back to view more than once, were *The Man Who Fell to Earth*, featuring David Bowie, and Andrei Tarkovsky's *Stalker* — the first film of his to be released since *Solaris*, which I had seen with Anna just before everything went to hell. After my nights in downtown Manhattan, I would get on the subway and head back to Coney Island.

The trains were appalling in those days. Covered with graffiti and filled with dangerous delinquents. I was already tempting death. Not just on the trains, but when I would arrive back at my ghetto housing project after drunkenly walking along the dark beach to get there, with my shoes in hand and my feet in the sand. Every now and then, I would be confronted by some murderous black hoodlum in the stairwell of the high rise. But before he could pull a knife or gun on me, his eyes would recognize the thousand yard stare in mine. When they saw that, they would leave me alone — some out of fear and others out of pity. Maybe they imagined that I had served in Vietnam and was, consequently, a psychotically hardened killer.

Oh, that was the other thing. In the future that I had seen, Nixon crushed the North Vietnamese. He burned them out of their jungles, not just with napalm, but ultimately with tactical nuclear weapons. Instead, on this timeline, he had withdrawn US forces from Vietnam in the most humiliating defeat suffered by this country since Korea. Soon, as the North Vietnamese invaded South Vietnam, and President Ford refused to resume American intervention, that war became the worst defeat in the history of the United States. There were other consequences of this that I found personally demoralizing. Rather than building up into a powerful revolutionary force, the Weather Underground, with which I still had some sympathy, lost their *raison d'être* and broad-based ideological appeal in society, such that they withered into a fringe terrorist group even more marginal than the New Age cults that had sprung up contemporaneously, in 1968 or 1969. In the four years between 1976 and 1980, each time another member of the Weather Underground turned him or herself in, I became more depressed and demoralized. It is not as if I identified with their ideology, I never really had — despite briefly funding them. However, I did see them as rebels against the intolerable status quo and shooting stars that portended a true revolution.

That revolution would never come, and the Communist revolution that I had foreseen in Iran was somehow subverted into the most bizarre theocratic Islamic 'revolution' — if one can even call something so regressive "revolutionary". Events with the Soviets in Afghanistan played out exactly as I had foreseen, with the same timeframe of 1978 to 1980. But in Iran, instead of Marxist proxies of the Soviet Union rising up against the Shah, these groups were marginalized and eventually co-opted by a much more virulent theocratic opposition committed to the Islamic fundamentalism of the Ayatollah Khomeini. When I saw Khomeini in Paris, surrounded by the international media, and read the disparaging CIA assessment of the Shah leaked to the press, then watched the Carter Administration repeatedly undermine Pahlavi, it was clear to me that I was neither paranoid nor narcissistic to believe that I had changed the course of history.

The data that Hal had passed onto the CIA from our sessions on the Soviet invasion of Iran had evidently inspired a plan to replace the Pahlavi regime with a so-called "Islamic Republic" that would contain Soviet Communism without risking a nuclear confrontation with the Shah who, not incidentally, never completed construction of the nukes that Nixon would have encouraged him to build. I was sickened by watching women forced under black veils, homosexuals being executed, and the sophisticated forward-looking Pahlavi regime replaced by draconian medieval laws against the sinful consumption of alcohol and erotic relations outside of marriage (which was now legal for nine year old girls, following the exemplar of Muhammad).

That I had a hand in this was appalling to me, and having saved the world from nuclear Armageddon was little consolation. I felt as if a world this absurdly warped ought to be set on fire. It broke my heart to see the Shah of Iran in exile, wasting away from cancer, less than a decade after that monumental pageantry at Persepolis — especially his unforgettable speech about Persian Imperial resurgence at the tomb of

Cyrus the Great. By 1979, when the CIA was at work destroying Iran, and what little remained of the radical left in America was surrendering to the state, I could barely tolerate watching the news. Instead, my television consumption turned into a cocktail of paranormal programs, both fictional and purportedly factual.

Since I moved to Coney Island, I had been watching reruns of the *Twilight Zone* late at night. To this was added the sequel of that TV series, *Night Gallery*, where Rod Serling would step into an art gallery full of creepy paintings and focus in on one as he delivered the opening narration for the night's episode. By the time I started viewing the *Night Gallery*, the early 1970s series *The Sixth Sense*, featuring Gary Collins as the Parapsychologist Dr. Lucas Darrow, had been repurposed and integrated into the show, with Rod Serling delivering introductions to what had once been episodes of this separate series. Paintings were produced to reflect the repurposed material. Then there was *The Outer Limits*, which with its harder science edge to its science fiction, appealed to what was left of the Physicist in me, as compared to the uncanny fantasy of *Twilight Zone* and *Night Gallery*. I also began religiously watching the non-fiction show *In Search Of*, where Leonard Nimoy hosted an exploration of various paranormal phenomena and mysteries of history, from ESP to Reincarnation, UFOs, Atlantis, and the Loch Ness Monster.

Somehow this visual carnival contributed to the atmosphere of living in Coney Island. So it was as much an immersion into the carnivalesque atmosphere of the place, as it was an escape from reality. There was something comforting about these four television shows, or five if you count *The Sixth Sense* as separate from other episodes of the *Night Gallery*. However limited their audience may have been, they still served to relatively normalize the bizarre horrors that were actually the element of my increasingly ethereal existence. They were also an antidote to the brooding seriousness of what would be my final writing project. *Invisible Imperium* was my working title for it.

Within the first year of becoming a fugitive, I had transformed my MA thesis on the Physics and Metaphysics of Free Will into a book called *Being Bound for Freedom*. Then there was *Faustian Futurism*. The third project, which I had spent most of my time on since relocating to Coney Island, was something like a dialectical product of the tension between the first two books. *Faustian Futurism* had been critical of Traditionalist Fascism in order to develop the concept of an alternative, Fascist Futurism. I had intended it as a tool in an attempt to infiltrate a hidden Fascist network that I believed may have been manipulating me, from my early childhood onwards. By contrast, *Invisible Imperium* was an exposé of the genealogy and structure of this Fascist shadow government, and a critique of its ideology and aims on the basis of the metaphysics, epistemology, and implicit ethics of *Being Bound for Freedom*.

Invisible Imperium was also meant to be a cathartic confrontation with the reality of my own life, or as much of it as I could piece together. When my research revealed that the CIA was constituted in 1947 from out of an OSS assimilation of General Reinhardt Gehlen's Nazi spy network in Eastern Europe, which was spearheaded by Ukrainians, I also unveiled the true identity and allegiance of both my aunt and my father. Thompson had told me that Otto Skorzeny was my aunt's commanding officer. He meant *after* the war. While Gehlen was busy helping the Americans build the CIA as a cold war weapon against Soviet Russia, Skorzeny had set up an organization of former SS officers, which was officially called ODESSA, but unofficially known by its code name, *Die Spinne* or "the Spider."

In addition to Gehlen Org assets in Eastern Europe, in 1946 ODESSA absorbed the remnants of the Intermarium organization masterminded by the Polish military tactician and statesman Józef Pilsudski. Also known as "Prometheism", in homage to the rebel titan Prometheus who was chained in the Caucasus mountains, the Promethean spirit of the movement can best be seen in the archeo-futuristic art of the Polish painter and sculptor Stanislaw Szukalski.

These advocates of the formation of a super-state stretching between the Baltic Sea, the Black Sea, and across the Caucasus to the Caspian Sea, were initially opposed to both the Germans and the Russians and were intent on defending their independence from both major powers. However, when Nazi Germany collapsed in 1945 and the Soviet Union invaded Eastern Europe and extended its territory in the Caucasus into northwestern Iran in 1946, even if it was over Pilsudski's dead body (he died in 1935), the partisans of Prometheism agreed to be integrated into the Spider's web of anti-Soviet resistance. This delivered even more assets into the hands of ODESSA, from anti-communist Ukrainian and Polish patriots all the way to Persian nationalists in the Soviet-occupied Iranian province of Azerbaijan, who, as heirs of Zarathustra, had been the southeastern most frontiersmen of the Prometheism project. Almost no one realized it was because of the network Pilsudski's Prometheism project had already established extending to the Caspian, that so many Poles fleeing, first Nazism and then Communism, were able to take refuge in Iran in the late 1940s.

The Spider played a significant role in planning and executing Operation Paperclip, the OSS and then CIA repatriation of thousands of Nazi scientists from various fields to the United States. They would become the bedrock of the American Military-Industrial Complex. The most prominent of these men, Dr. Werner von Braun, was put in charge of the Apollo program that successfully took America to the Moon based on project designs that he had originally drafted for Hitler. "Paperclip" referred to the fake dossiers manufactured to sanitize the record of repatriated Germans such as Von Braun, or the majority of his handpicked team at NASA who, like Kurt Debus, were also hard core Nazis. For example, it was hidden from the American public that Von Braun was an SS Major who used slave labor inside hollowed out mountains to build V-2 rockets for the purpose of targeting civilians in cities like London.

The men imported into the United States were at least as bad, if not worse, than the ones tried for war crimes at Nuremberg. Those who were prosecuted, and in some cases executed, were simply more dispensable than the brilliantly wicked ones worthy of being recruited by the USA. Certain very valuable Nazi scientists, such as Josef Mengele, were simply too blood-soaked to even attempt to sanitize with false dossiers. ODESSA arranged for these men to be resettled in Latin America rather than in North America. This was done with the full knowledge of the Nazi operatives who held key positions in the CIA from its inception. The Vatican also facilitated this relocation. Most went to Argentina, some to Chile, and a few to Mexico.

When I learned of this, it brought back a couple of childhood memories that were so disturbing that they had been totally buried in my subconscious. My aunt and uncle had taken me to Southern California, supposedly for a summer vacation. I think this was between second and third grade. We stayed in Los Angeles for about a week, where they took me to Disney Land and some of the Hollywood studios. But then, and this is the part of the memory that I had totally repressed, we drove down past San Diego and across the border to a coastal part of Baja, Mexico.

My uncle was very silent in the car, but my aunt told me that they were taking me to a "school for special children." Even now, it is a struggle to hold onto a few fragmentary memories of what happened there. What I *can* tell you is that the place was run by Germans. In fact, I don't remember a single Mexican from that brief excursion into Mexico. This "school" was a creepy old mansion that looked like a cross between an elegant chateau and a hunting lodge. It had lush, verdant gardens full of monarch butterflies. There were large, circular wood chandeliers inside the mansion. It was built atop a rocky promontory with steep cliffs diving into the waves of the Pacific Ocean.

I vaguely recall being corralled into a dungeon with other children there, and being forced to listen to the most horrific screams in the pitch dark before the stone cellar was shot through with artificial lightning that intermittently illuminated severed limbs and mangled corpses all around us. One of these other children, a little girl, huddled close to me throughout this and other similarly horrific experiences that we shared for what must have been several days. In retrospect, I realize that she looked an awful lot like Anna. I couldn't know for sure, because Anna never showed me pictures of her as a little girl. In fact, having cut off her family for reasons that were never clear to me, she refused to say very much at all about her childhood.

Rome was the locale of the other memory that came back to me through this research on Skorzeny's Spider and Gehlen's Organization. It was about a year after my uncle had died, so I was 11. My aunt had brought me with her to Rome, where we stayed at a hotel that was more like a rented apartment in a building with a courtyard where we would have breakfast. Over the arched gateway into the courtyard and the apartment complex as a whole, there was a frieze of Romulus and Remus sucking at the tits of the She Wolf. One day, after walking around the ruins of Capitoline Hill, where my aunt was able to tell me the most obscure and yet fascinating details about some of the monuments, we went to the Vatican to meet a man who had arranged to take us on a private tour of the catacombs.

He was a very intimidating dark haired gentlemen with a mustache and fencing scar, who had a knowing look on his face as he spoke with my aunt *in fluent German*, and a wicked glimmer in his eye when he looked at me. My aunt had saluted him when he arrived, but he quickly motioned for her to cut that out and gave her a warm hug with a kiss on both cheeks.

We descended into the dark underbelly of the Vatican, stepping over chains and warning signs that blocked off certain paths, and winding our way through rocky passages that became narrower with each turn. Our guide had a flashlight, which he would occasionally put under his chin when he looked at me. Man did he look creepy like that, especially with the scar. Only after doing the research for *Invisible Imperium* did I recognize that face. It was Otto Skorzeny, Hitler's master of Psychological Operations.

Skorzeny would point the light at various tombs cut into the rock, and full of the bones of ancient Romans. I clung closer and closer to my aunt, with my head pressing into her breasts, smelling her perfume mixed with the dense mildew of this place. There were cobwebs everywhere. At a certain point, Skorzeny turned off his flashlight. All I remember about the impenetrable darkness of that moment is that the smell of the place changed. Now, mixed with the perfume and mildew, there was a scent that vacillated between sulfur and cinnamon. There was also a sound, which I can only compare to a croaking of cicadas that was, in its own way, as melodious as birdsong. It made my heart flutter and my stomach quiver.

The next thing I remember is being back in the hotel room with my aunt that night. I found it strange that no one else was staying at this 'hotel', especially since it was the peak summer travel season. In any case, we had a furnished apartment with one bedroom and no neighbors. The maid who would serve us breakfast in the courtyard knew not to come to the apartment unless she was sure that we were out for the day. We were on the top floor, on a hilltop, with a spectacular view over Rome. I remember walking up to my aunt as she leaned out over the windowsill into the night air with the gauzy drapes blowing. Nikita drew me into her chest so that I could take in the night view of the ancient city with her.

I turned about between her and the window and looked up into her face, watching her gaze out over Rome before looking down into my eyes. She kissed my forehead, with the fingers of both hands wrapped around my head, as if she were drinking from a skull chalice. Then, with the window left open, she led me to the bed and sort of just fell into it while pulling my body down over hers. Nikita unbuttoned my shorts and I bent my knees as she pulled my underwear off. My flushed cheek pressed against her face – almost as warm as my cock, which was burning up like a branding iron.

She flipped me over, so that I was under her, and removed my shirt after unzipping and pulling her own dress off. She wasn't wearing any undergarments. Then she reached over to one of the bedside tables and pulled a strange clear flask out of the drawer, laying this next to us on the crumpled blanket. With a mischievous look in her eye, she started going down on me. When I tried to pull her body up a few times by the shoulders, so that she could sit on me, instead she swung around and straddled my face with her thighs as she continued to suck my hairless taught balls and prepubescent cock. She would occasionally place her fingers gently on my stomach, carefully sensing the quivering muscles.

Finally, her sucking felt so intensely pleasurable that it hurt. She noticed that I suddenly stopped playing with her dripping wet vulva and gripped her thighs as I squirmed as if to pull my cock out of her mouth. Then she quickly slipped the head of my cock into the opening of the flask's neck, while she held the bulbous part of it against my stomach. I looked down and saw my own cum for the first time as it spurted into the flask over and over again, while my legs trembled. The liquid was so warm that I could feel it through the glass pressing against my stomach. As soon as my cock stopped spurting, my aunt twisted the flask away so as not to spill it.

She pulled me close to her naked body under the silk sheets and cozy blanket, stroking my head and neck hypnotically and whispering in my ears until I fell asleep. That night I dreamt that a large grey owl was sitting in the windowsill staring at me as I lay in bed. The next morning, before Nikita woke up, I looked everywhere for the flask. It wasn't on the bedside table, and was nowhere to be found.

In any case, *Invisible Imperium* exposed the machinations of "the Spider" — a vast inter-continental Fascist network that was based in the deepest strata of the United States Military-Industrial and Intelligence Complex. I showed how their faction within the CIA was behind Charlie Manson, how he was a Frankenstein's monster that they were, at one point, planning to turn into a rock star and then into an American Hitler on a subsequently abandoned timeline that would have led to a race war by the 1980s. The whole Laurel Canyon phenomenon, and a lot of the psychedelic drug cults and ghetto drug dealing of the late 1960s, was manufactured to accelerate the decline of a decadently permissive society so as to drive the West toward what Spengler called "Caesarism" and what Yockey had elaborated on in *Imperium* (except that they did not share Yockey's view of the Russians). On the one hand, they were pouring accelerant on liberal-democratic America and giving the children matches to eventually set it on fire. On the other hand, they were working to defeat the Soviet Union and bring about its collapse. Once the latter was accomplished, they could finish the job of destroying American society from within by promoting identity politics and a radical leftist agenda that could only end with the violent disintegration of the United States.

The Spider hoped that something like the Confederacy would reemerge from out of this collapse, the largest chunk of the Former USA, and that they would be in a position to govern this American rump state more or less directly. They would then interlink it, NATO-style, with Fascist states that they planned to carve out of the Eastern Bloc of the collapsed USSR, with Ukraine as the backbone of the Fourth Reich's European territories. All of this was merely stage-setting, a rolling out of the red carpet for the denizens of the Atlantean Underworld who planned to resurface as angelic saviors and act as the true founders of the "Thousand-Year Reich."

Around the time that I finished *Invisible Imperium*, a large black dog had started to follow me along the beach and the boardwalk at night. This bitch became so persistent that she eventually tailed me all the way to the door of my apartment. She did this several times before I finally let her in late one night in the summer of 1980, after staggering home again along the beach drunk and barefoot, with my feet skirting the tide and the bitch running along beside me, imprinting her paws into the wet sand. When the initial liquor-induced slumber wore off, around 4am, I noticed that she had gotten up and was walking toward the door to my apartment, repeatedly looking back at me. I had fallen asleep in my clothes. For some reason that I could not explain to myself, as I got up to walk the dog out of the building I grabbed the black metal urn of Anna's ashes, which, as you may recall, was embossed with the Trident of Poseidon.

The black bitch led me out of my building and back down to the beach. It was a couple of hours before dawn, and the only lights anywhere were those of the Wonder Wheel, which oddly enough, had been left on. This hound goaded me along the shoreline from Coney Island to Brighton Beach, and then she stopped dead almost exactly where Anna's body had been recovered. She looked up at me insistently, barking a few times. I took the lid off the urn, and carefully held it down at the edge of the tide, allowing a little bit of the ocean foam to wash into the ashes. Then, I dug my fingers into the urn and started smearing the wet ash all over my face and neck. I stripped stark naked, doing the same thing with the rest of my body until I was caked in Anna's remains. The black bitch watched, almost silently, but for occasional panting and muffled moaning. Then I walked into the water, and I kept walking. It felt cool compared to the warmth of the summer night. After swimming some ways out into the Atlantic, I turned around and looked back at the beach.

Perhaps I would have come to my senses and swum back, with all the force of a man who decides to cling to life at the last moment. But what I saw on the beach made me swim out even further. Two chalky white-faced tall men in black suits and black ties, wearing fedora hats, had walked up behind the now whimpering dog. One of them was carrying a knife that glistened in the full moon's light. The other seemed to be opening a violin case, which he laid down on the sand. Then he grabbed the black bitch and just as suddenly, the other man slit the dog's throat and I saw her legs buckle under her. She collapsed next to the discarded urn of Anna's ashes, which I had emptied onto my own body. Even though I was too far away to clearly make out their eyes, I could feel the two men in black staring at me menacingly. I swam out so far away from them, that by the time I stopped I knew that I would never make it back.

CHAPTER 9

WHITE DEVILS

y lungs burned when the water filled them, and I could feel my heart stop as I suffocated under the waves. Instead of rising up out of my body, I felt myself fall out of it through my feet with a sensation similar to that of falling dreams. I saw my corpse slowly sinking in the water above me, as I was pulled out into the Atlantic and down into the ocean depths with great speed and fluidity. Before long I saw the glowing blue window portals of a metallic, perfectly cigar-shaped vehicle with no fins or wings. I passed right through one of these windows and found myself haunting the inside of this vessel. It was speeding up through the ocean, surrounded by a membrane of some kind that eliminated any resistance from the water. The crew consisted of those tall, Nordic types. They were manning controls with glowing, multicolored lights that stood out against the relatively colorless grey and blue-grey surfaces inside the ship, which complemented the livid skin-tight uniforms and platinum blond hair of these men and women. I thought of Cybele.

The earth could soon be seen out the windows, first as a breathtakingly gigantic vista, and then as a shrinking blue planet. Meanwhile, the Moon kept getting larger. Eventually, the craters on the bright side of it could be seen in detail. Then we went over the top of the Moon and gracefully descended onto the dark side of it. As we approached the surface, I could see lights twinkling inside a large crater. When we got even closer, there was the stunning sight of a vast array of geometric buildings that appeared to be made out of some kind of poured stone. They gave me the impression of concrete bunkers, but on a titanic scale and built of something more like the precisely-interlocked polygonal megaliths of ruins in Peru or Bolivia. Unlike the majority of these structures, a few of the most gigantic ones were spherical. There was also a very tall obelisk-shaped tower, like the Washington Monument, with blinking lights on top of it.

When the crew disembarked from the vessel inside a huge hanger, I followed several of them as they exited the spaceport and made their way down a long hallway with a ceiling that tapered in tiers, like a key pattern. This hallway terminated at what appeared to be a tube station, where they waited for a monorail, like the one that I had ridden with Cybele, levitating slightly above the track that it pulled up on. This train took them to a station that was connected to a gargantuan command center, with ceilings that were at least two hundred feet high, and walls that were covered in display screens apparently connected to hulking banks of machinery studded with colorfully lit control panels. It was clear that something was generating a local gravity field in this city, equal to the gravity of Earth.

The atmosphere and technology was essentially the same as what I had witnessed of the undersea world during my remote viewing work for Naval Intelligence at the World Trade Center. We had known that these 'people' were going up to the Moon, and had glimpsed this city that I was now in, or at least one like it. However, it had been even harder to see anything clearly here than it was to clairvoyantly perceive the facilities built into the continental shelf and hollowed out mountain ranges under the oceans. It was as if we had been psychically blocked from exploring the Moon, especially its dark side, where cities like this one were located inside large craters. We could only look through a glass darkly at what I was experiencing at first hand now. I recall that on one occasion I hesitated reporting to Jack that I had seen a group of these people practicing Yoga *asanas*. The men and women striking these poses in perfect synchronicity with one another were stark naked, and didn't have an ounce of fat on their perfectly sculpted bodies. They moved as if they were the limbs of a single mind, with their gazes hypnotically fixed on something beyond the Moon, the Earth, or even the stars.

The most disturbing encounter that I had during one of these Naval Intelligence sessions took place when I was noticed by one of the Nordic supermen working here. He was psychically alerted to my presence, and even seemed to be looking at me as I remote viewed him and his surroundings. "You shouldn't be here," he 'said' *telepathically*. "What *is* this place?" I asked. "It is where we harvest the souls of people who have perished." I was appalled at this answer and I asked, "*Harvest* them?" He replied, "Yes. Our perpetual motion machines run on souls."

When he said this I got a mental image of all manner of 'intelligent' machines with the vital energy of what *had been* 'people' trapped inside them, powering them like batteries. "For *how long?!*" I asked, exasperated. "Until they wear out," he said. "*Wear out?!*" I exclaimed. "Yes. The psychical constitution of a being can only sustain itself for so long under such conditions. It wears thin in isolation from sensuous reality, and under a pattern of activity that is so routinized." Deeply demoralized by this answer, I questioned him in dismay, "Then even souls die?" Despite the fact that I mumbled this more than half rhetorically, the Nordic superman explained, "Everything can be torn apart in time. Nothing is eternal. Nothing and no one."

That conversation had been like a half forgotten dream until I found myself here, in what Tibetans call the *bardo* state between death and rebirth, face to face with these self-appointed harvesters of souls. Fortunately, I had not gone "into the light." From what I was able to gather that is how they trap souls and successfully lure some of them into those machines. I was wary of getting too close to these contraptions, although I managed to get a good sense of some of their functions while I wandered in this place for what seemed to be days (given the lack of an atmosphere, it was a lot harder to keep time, especially in this disoriented postmortem state). The most burdensome task performed by these diabolical devices was the formulation of projected futures. These could be modeled in a high degree of detail, and then altered with a view to the adjustment of variables, back on Earth, with a magnitude sufficient to redirect the trajectory of human history. These *lunatics* were aiming to use this technology in order to resurrect their lost Atlantis over the ruins that they planned to make of modern terrestrial societies.

Even if I was terrified of looking directly into the quasi-sentient and inhuman intelligence of these devices that were dependent upon the repurposing of what had once been human souls, I could still form a fairly sophisticated picture of the future that was being projected. For that, all I needed to do was to telepathically penetrate the minds of those who were interacting with these unholy machines. This was easier said than done, because the 'people' up here had much more of a sense of when their minds were being probed than ordinary folks on Earth did. But I had practiced this when, at the behest of Naval Intelligence, I was trying to read the same people stationed in their submarine facilities or undersea cities.

The more I spied on the thoughts and emotions of those involved with the project of reemerging into the open on Earth, the more precognitive glimpses I began to get of this possible future. I was no longer simply reconstructing it analytically with my intellect. This future became something more like a remote viewing target. In the end, I was drawn there as if by a magnet. Instead of merely traversing vast distances of intra-lunar space in the astral state, I was projected many decades into the future. The intelligence that I had produced to foresee and prevent the Soviet invasion of Iran had not averted the apocalyptic return of the Atlantean exiles. Instead, it had only changed the conditions under which their occulted Leviathan would surface.

I do not intend for this to become a lecture on the history of the future. But without painting a picture of the first half of the next century in at least broad brushstrokes, the images that I beheld of the second half as I wandered the bardo state would be much more incomprehensible to you than they were to me. You see, somehow when I puzzled at one or another scene, the historical factors that produced it would come to me with the quality of a vague recollection of things once learned but forgotten. So I will append my recollection of these things to this account in the form of an epilogue, titled "How the Modern World Ended." Reading that epilogue and then rereading what I am about to share with you will help to make sense out of the bizarre scenes that I witnessed of life on this planet from about the year 2048 until 2112, when the time barrier was broken so badly that chronological history became meaningless.

The first hair-raising image, which I beheld in the bardo state, was the inside of a boardroom in a skyscraper that was one of many buildings with an Art Deco aesthetic, but constructed on the titanic scale of the futuristic metropolitan architectural drafts of Hugh Ferriss. It was built on highlands that overlooked the skyscrapers of Manhattan, as they rose out of the waves of the Atlantic ocean that pounded against the sides of them and washed through the channels that were once the streets of this city. In this boardroom, a group of businessmen were seated around a long rectangular table that shone like a slab of polished dark grey stone. Its surface reflected the sunlit, glinting gold in a metal sculpture of a chimerical cross between a dragon, a bird, and a dog. It stood out from the wall in relief and somehow periodically morphed its shape. The men all wore black suits and ties, and they had gaunt faces with high cheekbones and chiseled Nordic features. On the table in front of them was a feast that they were about to dig into — the crispy cooked carcass of a jet black dog on her back, with her limbs in the air. The bitch's stomach was sliced open to reveal garnished stuffing. I was left with the distinct impression that this was not a typical business lunch of any kind. Rather, it was more akin to a ritual sacrifice intended to inaugurate some great undertaking.

The next image involved the attempt made by the tall Nordics to reshape the ruins of the modern world into a simulacrum of their lost Atlantis. The Atlanteans wanted to replace the "degenerate" cult of the individual in the modern West, which they saw as definitive of its terminal decline, with a hierarchy of human *types* that would constitute an organic state in an integral and co-dependent fashion, the way that a brain, heart, and limbs are all integral to a single human organism. The social organism of Atlantis was held together by telepathic and telekinetic control, both from the top down and across the collective of each caste.

I saw them inside of a blue-grey marble building with awe-inspiringly tall ceilings. It reminded me of the interior of the front of the International Building, behind the statue of Atlas, at Rockefeller Center, but it was more titanic and had a waterfall. The building was an administrative center or base of operations embedded in an increasingly hostile urban landscape. I focused on one woman in particular, who was walking up a very broad stairway. She had the same beautiful brutality to her build as the rest of them did, but I noticed something else in her posture and expression. Her strong legs were almost trembling, and she looked overwhelmed.

I could see into her mind, which was uncharacteristically disarrayed for an Atlantean — perhaps even a bit frantic. What I saw were buildings exploding into shards of glass onto sidewalks emptied out by martial law and curfews. The terrorism was getting worse, and the insurgents responsible for it were as elusive as ghosts. The Atlanteans had wanted to be received as angels, but now they were losing the battle for hearts and minds. There was a shocking fragility to her. What happened next was truly startling. She *saw me*, there on those steps. She stopped dead, and looked straight into my eyes like a startled predator. Then she went to grab my arm, and as her hand passed through my spectral form I could hear her wordless, desperate plea inside my mind: "We're not devils! *You* can still save us."

No, they were not the ones who looked like devils. Although, appearances can certainly be deceiving. I *did see* creatures that looked like devils or demonic elves. These were the biomechanical robots that, back in my Naval Intelligence work, I had learned 'manned' the Atlantean vessels and dealt with the abductees. Cloaked inside a hollowed out asteroid, there was a facility where, by means of some mad science that was more like alchemy, these artificial beings were gestating and growing in glowing incubators. They were hairless, with bulbous heads and pointy chins with hardly a trace of mouth or nose. They had slender torsos and freakishly long, skeletal limbs. The hands had only four fingers, ending in long black nails. Their feet were bird-like, and looked as if they could gut a man. Their eyes were almond-shaped and huge. The whole place was permeated with an awful smell that reminded me of sulfur and cinnamon, or smoldering cardboard that has gotten soaked. When I was up close to an incubator, wincing as I took in the shape of these hideous grey things, one of them opened its eyelids. The blackness therein was so deep and vast that it felt as if my soul had been captured by the event horizon of a singularity. This may have been because their bodies were shells or suits designed, not only for navigating space, but for penetrating past epochs.

In fact, the technology and techniques of time travel that I witnessed from the late 21st century and into the early 22nd century convinced me that history did not have to end this way. I vowed to go back, and to elaborate a vision that would preempt this horrific future. As I began to be pulled back to New York in 1980, as if by a gravitational force aligned with my ardent intention and implacable will, I caught a glimpse of the life that I was about to be born into – a moment from a possible future different from the one that I had wandered through after drowning.

...I was solemnly shaking hands with a man of towering stature and august countenance. The business suit was meant to be disarming, but somehow it made him look even more out of place. We were in a great hall that felt like the General Assembly of the United Nations, but this was some other organization. Its insignia was embossed on the podium and emblazoned on flags to the sides of it: four red flames forming a cross with a Swastika spinning at the center of it, inside of a white circle, set against an indigo blue field studded with the constellations of Pisces and Aquarius.

My sense was that we were in Paris, because in my mind's eye I could see that as I was delivering introductory remarks to the audience in the run up to his speech he was being driven up to the Trocadero of the Palais de Chaillot in a black limousine. There was a red carpet reception. The press were being held back vigilantly by a very nervous armed contingent. They looked like they were holding their breath the whole time he made his way down toward the front of the assembly chamber and ascended the dais where I was awaiting him.

I straightened my spine as much as possible and shook his hand as firmly as I could. His other arm locked around my elbow as he stared straight into my eyes and smiled. Very few could have borne gazing into those bottomless pools of sky blue, but it was in the way the smile broke up that stone cold face that I saw something truly extraordinary: profoundly concerned, but faithful hope. It was as if it made his platinum hair hang more softly around his head and shoulders, blunting the edges.

The streets of the world's cities were filled with shards of shattered glass and the smoke of mobs ablaze with rage, trying to burn themselves out before they joined the others who were already wasting away of starvation and disease. To many of them this was the apocalypse, and I was "the Antichrist" who had struck a Faustian bargain to free the Titans from Tartarus and let them loose upon the Earth once more. Yet, in that moment, when Apollyon and I locked arms and he opened his eyes to me through his smile, I saw that he was risking just as much as any one of us. Nobody knew how this story would end. We were rewriting our future. He was rewriting the Atlantean heritage, helping me to reweave the web of our shared destiny.

...I raised my head from out of my hands. The sound of car horns had disturbed my weeping. As my eyes opened, I saw the taxis that were causing the commotion. Then, struggling with the disorientation of one who emerges from the deepest and longest of dreams, I realized that I was sitting on the steps of St. Patrick's Cathedral. Judging by the style of the checkered cabs, and by the attire of all the pedestrians, I seemed to have returned to New York — except that it was no longer summer. A light snow was falling and the tears froze on my cheeks. Perhaps only six or seven months had gone by. It was early 1981. There were some discarded, partly crushed boxes that suggested Valentine's day might have just gone by.

At first I was ashamed to be sitting on these public steps in such a wretched condition, like one of the many homeless men huddled on them through most of the late 1970s. Then, when I went to cross the street, I realized that no one could see me. Almost no one. As I stood beneath the gaze of Atlas, the King of Atlantis, I had the most uncanny sense that the eyes set in that implacable black face were staring down hard at me with an expression between indignation and expectation.

I walked down Rockefeller Plaza and leaned against the wall over the ice skating rink to contemplate the statue of Prometheus soaring through the ring of zodiacal constellations with his stolen flame in hand. The inscription from Aeschylus engraved above him read: "Prometheus, teacher in every art, brought the fire that hath proved to mortals a means to mighty ends." The ice was empty, but for a single woman practicing her figure skating with the grace of an Olympic gymnast. She was ice dancing to Jimi Hendrix's rendition of "All Along the Watchtower." As my eyes ran over the contours of her beautiful body, I knew that it was just about time to be born again.

HOW THE MODERN
WORLD ENDED

Their flying saucers never landed. They stepped out of black limousines. This was no "alien invasion." To the eyes and ears of most survivors, who had endured decades of horror and hitherto unimaginable ugliness, the Atlanteans were mesmerizingly beautiful and captivatingly charismatic. They spoke both English and Mandarin flawlessly, in that hypnotic — almost melodic — tone of voice characteristic of their kind. What ought to have been even more shocking and incredible is the fact that they looked like Nordic supermodels, with the build of Olympic swimmers and the height of basketball stars.

That should have given people pause, and sounded an alarm — at least in the scientific community. But the truth is that most folks were so weary, traumatized, and suspended on the brink of despair that they almost unquestioningly welcomed the Atlanteans who came offering guidance into a new world of "sustainable peace and prosperity." The Prometheist rebels, who took a very different view, had their own name for Earth's putative saviors, the "White Devils." Whatever one wants to call them, they would never have been able to consolidate control over this planet if the modern world had not been demolished before their arrival.

So thoroughly demolished in fact that hardly anyone bothered to ask why these "Space Brothers (and Sisters)" had deceptively passed themselves off as denizens of the planet Venus when they manipulated quite a number of "Contactees" back in the 1950s and 60s. Granted, they did have bases both beneath the surface of Venus and on satellites orbiting that planet. But these were minimal compared to their cities on Mars or even their massive presence on Earth's own Moon, so they could hardly be justified in introducing themselves as "Venusians." If anything, they were Martians — with tens of millennia of civilizational history on Mars, of which the "Atlantean" culture that they eventually established on Earth was but a faint echo. Perhaps it was not lost on some of the Christians who saw all of this as the coming of the Antichrist that Venus, when it appears as the "morning star" rather than in the evening, is also called "Lucifer."

The Chinese made a cynical calculation in their typically utilitarian fashion. Their manned missions to the Moon, beginning in the late 2020s, had confirmed what orbital reconnaissance revealed even earlier: the occulted world of the Other People, constituted by survivors from Atlantis, largely based inside the mountains and under the lakes of Antarctica, and served by a Fascist breakaway civilization deeply entrenched within the American Military-Industrial-Intelligence complex. This gave the Chinese policymaking elite lead time to consider the question of what to do in the event that these Atlanteans were to reveal themselves. A cost/benefit analysis concluded that they should sell out humanity, and even volunteer Chinese power projection and authoritarian pacification in the service of the "elder race" by framing them, in Confucian terms, as wise ancestors or even Immortals — the "dragon kings and phoenix queens" who, in human prehistory, governed Earth in harmony with the "Law of Heaven."

By the 2040s the Chinese, who naturally had the highest IQ of any ethnic group on Earth, were using state mandated germ-line genetic engineering on a population-wide basis to increase this already high IQ to superhuman levels. They were also pursuing radical life extension by means of biotechnology. So they hoped to easily integrate into Atlantis, even if it meant playing a subordinate role as compared to whites in the West — who were obviously the closest genetic kindred of these Nordic supermen. After all, they had a huge advantage over the West, and over Russia, insofar as their population did not subscribe to the Judeo-Christian "revelation" that would be exposed as a manipulative fabrication after the "Disclosure" event of the mid 21st century. This meant that they would not suffer the violent social chaos that had already been tearing the West apart even before the archeological sites on Mars were revealed by mainstream media, together with the narrative of human 'prehistory' that their archives contained. These revelations that acted to destroy faith in revelation, whether of an Evangelical, Orthodox, or Catholic kind, poured so much accelerant on the already combustible social tensions in the West that sheer chaos reigned for some years in America, Europe, and Russia, while China was able to present itself as the most orderly society on Earth. This allowed the Chinese to become, for the Atlanteans, a managerial class akin to the Raj that had collaborated with the British colonizers to sell out the people of India. The Chinese had, in fact, positioned themselves to become middle men for the "Ancestors" as early as 2020 when they played a key role in engineering and unleashing COVID-19 at their Wuhan lab.

The economists, financiers, and policy planners who imagined that things would eventually go back to "normal" after the Coronavirus pandemic of 2020–21 were as deluded by the mirage of modernity as everyone else. Their faith in infinite growth, and in the liberal-democratic form of society sustained by capitalism, was shattered by many subsequent emergencies and convergent catastrophes. By the late 2030s, even the most levelheaded people were having trouble believing that this chain of events was nothing more than a long stroke of exceptionally bad luck. Whether they imagined that it was the wrath of God or that the hidden hand belonged to all-too-human conspira-tors, these apparently 'natural' catastrophes seemed designed to bring the modern world to an end.

It is surprising that so few people noticed that these several dec-ades of mysterious "misfortune" in the early to mid 21st century also effectively averted humanity's headlong plunge into the vortex of the Technological Singularity that John von Neumann had conceptual-ized, and that was subsequently predicted by many futurists. Certain elements of the envisioned Singularity did materialize. In fact, some revolutionary technologies rose to meet challenges posed by these so-called 'natural' catastrophes, and the way for others to predominate was paved by the disasters. For example, the pandemics brought with them a repeated disruption of labor of all kinds, increasingly serious concerns about contamination at industrial plants, as well as the huge spike in demand for home delivery of goods to a quarantined popula-tion. One cannot be faulted for wondering if it was more than merely fortuitous that this took place during the same decade as the revolu-tion in Robotics and Nanotechnology, and just after the development of viable drone delivery.

By far the most significant consequence of the approach toward the Technological Singularity was the serious engagement with spec-tral phenomena that was forced upon those mainstream scientists and engineers who skirted its event horizon. This took place in three main contexts, the quest for Artificial Intelligence, projects aimed at cybernetic integration of AI with humans using nanotechnology, and the attempt to genetically re-engineer significant aspects of the hu-man organism. In all of these cases, scientists engaged in research and development at well-funded and prestigious institutions were forced to confront, and ultimately to accept, empirical evidence for the kinds of phenomena that marginalized parapsychologists had already been studying for well over a century.

The closer AI researchers got to generating something like human consciousness inside of a computer system, the more their engineering projects were plagued by inexplicable and "spooky" manifestations of apparent telepathy and telekinesis on the part of the emergent mind of the machine. This became much worse when nanotechnology was used to transform certain human test subjects into cyborgs connected to AI systems that were intended to augment their cognitive functioning and afford these people the possibility of experiencing networked communication and information processing. What this resulted in was an enhancement of latent extrasensory perception, which the researchers were initially very reluctant to acknowledge. Eventually, however, they realized that cybernetic technology could be used to enhance the fidelity of clairvoyance, including precognitive clairvoyance, to such an extent that it had significant applications of interest to various industries. By 2035, clairvoyant precognitive cyborgs hooked to AI computer systems were being used, for example, to record high fidelity three-dimensional films of future terrorist attacks far enough in advance that they could be prevented by counter-terrorism units.

Finally, in the area of genetic engineering, researchers ran into anomalous mutations that forced them to recognize the existence of non-material information structures that play a key role in morphological development together with efficient causal mechanisms such as DNA. As cloning became more widespread, exceptionally strong telepathy and even shared memory among clones proved impossible to deny. Anomalies encountered in large scale births of what were supposed to have been designer babies also forced a recognition of the age-old phenomenon of psychokinetic "maternal impressions" resulting in deformity.

By the late 2030s, the social impact of mainstream scientific recognition of Extrasensory Perception (ESP) and Psychokinesis (PK) was already catastrophic. The court system began to be plagued with cases of individuals claiming that their nasty neighbors, jilted lovers, business rivals and so forth had subjected them to jinxes and hexes resulting either in property damage or physical harm or both. There were even cases of people claiming that their memories of being murdered in a past life allowed them to identify the murderer who had, thus far, escaped justice. A few people who claimed to be reincarnated inventors even tried to convince judges to reinstate their rights to the patents that they had drawn up in a past incarnation. What was even worse was the reaction of religious fundamentalists to all of this. They considered mainstream scientific acceptance of ESP and PK, and its consequent application in various areas of government, such as law enforcement, to be tantamount to an institutionalization of Satanic black magic and witchcraft. Armed mobs rose up against the reign of the "Antichrist", exacerbating already serious social tension to the point of mass hysteria.

However, on the whole, the socio-political and economic consequences of the various pandemics, eruptions, earthquakes, tsunamis, droughts, famines and other contrived disasters, prevented humanity from being captured by the event horizon of the Technological Singularity. Instead, the denizens of Earth now orbited ominously around that dark star. Whether we would finally dare to venture into it, and to discover if another world is possible on the other side of the looking glass, appeared to be the question at the crux of the conflict between the Promethean resistance and the "White Devils" that they see as the warders of this prison planet. What I found most appalling as I surveyed this situation, is how many of the technologies that I had invented in my life as Tesla were used in order to bring about the destruction of the modern world that these devices were designed to further develop.

Several units of an oscillator capable of triggering artificial earthquakes had been attached to long metal spikes that were driven down into the fault line under the Cumbre Vieja volcano on the island of La Palma. This was used to trigger an earthquake that caused a third of the volcano, which was already almost dislodged from the rest of it by a fissure, to collapse into the Atlantic Ocean. The force of the earthquake and eruption, when combined with the amount of displaced volcanic rock, resulted in a tsunami hundreds of meters high. It took about nine hours for this tidal wave to cross the North Atlantic Ocean before smashing into the skyscrapers of Manhattan and drowning other coastal cities in America. The same technique was used by divers who drove these spikes fitted with oscillators into the Cascadia Subduction Zone, a fault line in the Pacific Ocean just off the coast of the Pacific Northwest of the Former United States. The resulting 9.0 earthquake and attendant tsunami destroyed Vancouver, Seattle, and Portland, the three largest and most culturally sophisticated cities of the nascent Republic of Cascadia.

The flooding produced by these catastrophes was only temporary, but the engineers of the Neo-Atlantean Apocalypse employed other inventions of mine to produce more lasting flooding, and also droughts and forest fires. Several hidden arrays of antenna similar to the one that I constructed at Shoreham were used to shock the ionosphere of the Earth with electrical energy, superheating it in certain places at carefully calibrated intervals. I had written about how this could be used as a means to bring the weather under control, for the benefit of farmers and in order to avoid natural disasters. Instead, this system, which had been named HAARP or High-frequency Active Auroral Research Project, was deployed to the opposite effect – to engineer *seemingly* 'natural' disasters and to devastate agriculture, thereby leading to an appalling global famine.

Africa and other parts of the third and fourth world imported the majority of their food from North America. Once farms in the Former USA and Canada were suffering from droughts and forest fires, North Americans were struggling to produce enough for themselves and had no surplus to export. This meant the starvation of hundreds of millions of Africans and other non-whites in the global south. But the most catastrophic damage from the use of HAARP was from the hurricanes and other super storms, such as tornadoes, dust storms, and typhoons that it unleashed.

The worst flooding was created neither by the oscillator nor by HAARP, but through a secret use of my directed energy Teleforce device to shatter the ice sheets over Antarctica and Greenland in the early 2040s. Once the largest pieces of these ice caps were turned into ice cubes, they melted at an appalling rate – much faster than even the most alarmist prognosticators of global warming had predicted. Instead of global warming, the result was a plunge into a new Ice Age. The freshwater from the massive amounts of melting ice altered the salinity in the Atlantic Ocean, and the North Atlantic Conveyor belt shut down. This pump, which brought warm water up from the Caribbean along the coasts of North America and Western Europe, was dependent upon the density of saltwater in order to function. After the North Atlantic current stopped warming the coastal waters of New York, New England, Spain, France, and Britain, the polar region of the northern hemisphere expanded southwards by hundreds of kilometers. Not only were cities like New York permanently flooded by a precipitous sea level rise, they were rendered uninhabitable on account of extreme cold. Everything north of Virginia in America and north of the Mediterranean coast in Europe was covered in snow that never melted. Conditions in the Faustian World became Arctic — or Antarctic. The Atlanteans, who had burrowed stealthily in Antarctica for so many centuries, would thrive in it.

Fortunately, my inventions had nothing whatsoever to do with the genetically engineered pandemics. Those who were shocked out of their complacency by the Coronavirus pandemic of 2020–2022 could hardly have imagined that it would only be the first of many such catastrophes to fundamentally alter the human form of life. These pandemics became seasonal, flaring up in one or another region during optimal weather conditions. Eventually, the viruses eliminated many of the oldest, weakest, and most vulnerable people from the world's population.

What is worse, is that as the appalling death-toll mounted, and attempts at developing an effective vaccine continued to meet with failure, the widespread treatment of respiratory symptoms such as ear, nose, throat, and bronchial infections with antibiotics eventually resulted in herd immunity to antibiotics. Bacteria resistant to antibiotics flourished in the worldwide population, and antibiotic medicine ultimately collapsed as an effective treatment for *any* infections whatsoever. Millions of people began to die of infections that had been easily treatable in the 20th century.

If any sizeable percentage of the population had known that the majority of these viruses, beginning with the COVID-19 pandemic, were biological weapons engineered in a laboratory, perhaps public outrage would have militated against such a dire outcome. Unfortunately, those who presented evidence of the artificial structure of these super flus and super colds were relegated to the fringes of public discourse and branded "conspiracy theorists." That is, until some of these pandemics began to clearly discriminate between different ethnicities.

However, once it became clear that a disproportionate number of people with a particular cluster of genes were becoming victims of certain of these viruses, the socio-economic crisis was already so acute and established political systems had become so dysfunctional, that any attempt to hold suspect nations or their governments responsible proved to be futile. The institutionalization of social distancing and the effectively permanent prohibition of large gatherings also severely constrained the possibility of political protest against the perpetrators of genocide by means of biological warfare. As bio-warfare became a fact of life, it was increasingly used with impunity on the battlefield in parts of the world where failed states began to proliferate, and the ethnic groups involved in these conflicts turned on one another. Africans, Arabs, Jews, Turks, and Kurds all used biological weapons against each other.

The mass displacement of people by every manner of natural disaster also contributed to ethnic conflict and genocide, and served to further spread disease. By the 2030s, there were illegal migrations taking place on a scale that dwarfed the crisis of Middle Eastern and African migration of Muslims into Europe in the second decade of the 21st century, following the manufactured civil wars in Syria and Libya. This second and more serious wave of illegal mass migration took place in a much different sociopolitical atmosphere than the first wave. Leftist "anti-colonial" identity politics, and the inculcation of white guilt upon which it was dependent, had run their course by the late 2030s. The abject humiliation suffered by working class whites at the hands of "social justice" warriors during the dozen years of the Harris Administration initially gratified radical leftists, who cheered on the destruction of historical monuments to men like Thomas Jefferson and Winston Churchill. Eventually, they even went so far so to publicly burn books written by "racist intellectuals" such as Aristotle and Nietzsche. This changed, however, once the black and brown people with whom they claimed to be acting in solidarity began to implement Sharia Law and other regressively discriminatory governmental policies. Even white (and Jewish) leftists were silently horrified by 2039, when the sale of alcohol—including wine and beer—was banned, and nightclubs were shut down, in cities such as Detroit, Paris, and Berlin, where the Muslim call to prayer could be heard five times a day.

The Islamic demographic conquest of Europe had one unintended consequence that contributed to catalyzing the Fascist reaction against it. Unintended, that is, by the witless Leftist tools who were used as proxies to empower Muslims, not by the Spiders who were pulling the puppet strings of the Islamist Arabs, Turks, Pakistanis, and Africans as they put the finishing touches on a worldwide Web. Once major media outlets began to be controlled by the Muslim demographic conquerors of Europe, who also overpowered the "Social Justice Warriors" that facilitated their takeover, rabid Anti-Zionists totally deconstructed the post World War II narrative about the Holocaust of European Jews by Nazi Germany.

The new narrative, which even European whites on the Left were not allowed to challenge, for fear of being called "racist Zionists" by brown-skinned Muslims, was that the concentration camps that Germany built in Central and Eastern Europe were internment and labor camps no different from the ones that the United States used to intern Japanese Americans. They only turned into "death camps" when the Allied powers, especially Britain, used their Air Forces to bomb the train lines that were supplying these labor camps with food and medicine. It is then that the laborers were afflicted with starvation and contracted diseases such as cholera and typhus. In order to contain these epidemics, the bodies of starved and diseased inmates were sterilized in ovens and burnt to ash. Forensic evidence was presented that the "gas chambers" were simply de-lousing rooms where pesticides were used to kill disease-spreading lice. Finally, it was reported that the *number* of Jews who died in these camps *due to the deliberate Allied engineering of starvation and disease* was 2.4 million at most, not "six million" as the catechism of the "Zionist controlled media" had alleged.

Perhaps the European Left ought to have considered the fact that the Muslims they empowered were led by Arab organizations that, since the 1950s, had been under the control of the Spider's agents in Egypt, Syria, Iraq, and elsewhere throughout the Islamic world, including "Occupied Palestine." By the late 2030s, most Europeans hated Israel and the Jews as much as they resented their new Muslim overlords. That Jewry had manipulated and deceived them for nearly a century was the only thing that they agreed with their new masters about. Germans who, for several generations, had been browbeaten into a sense of collective guilt from childhood, underwent an especially vehement turnabout. It was as if a switch flipped inside them. The resurgent German Right faced little to no resistance from the Left, which by now was appalled by Sharia Law zones in Berlin, Munich, and other cities dominated by rabidly Anti-Semitic Turks.

The dynamics of the situation in North America were somewhat different, but not much better on the whole. Canada, with its significant Muslim population in metropolitan areas, saw similar struggles as parts of Europe did. What happened in Toronto and Montreal was a pale reflection of the sociopolitical chaos in London and Paris (Montreal was eventually saved by the secession of Quebec). In what had been the United States of America, religion was less of a factor than race, although the nascent Europe-based Caliphate did try to convert significant numbers of African Americans to Islam and was partly successful in doing so. The various natural catastrophes suffered by America, from the pandemics to the earthquakes, tsunamis, super storms, droughts, forest fires, and famines, all served as resonance amplifiers to intensify social discord and racial conflict.

As resources became increasingly scarce, and devastated cities were left lawless by the Leftist defunding of putatively "racist" police departments, gang violence spread from out of ghettos and catalyzed a race war. This race war, which erupted in earnest during the third term of President Kamala Harris (2028–2032), was not only a struggle pitting blacks against whites, but also a conflict between Latinos and blacks, and a vengeance of hardworking Asians suffering large-scale property-damage against both blacks and Latinos. The Chinatown and Koreatown districts of large American cities were as integral to the conflict as the borders between black and white or black and Latino neighborhoods. There, the dictates of Asian mafias and the "protection" provided by them became the de-facto law and order.

Beginning in 2033, repeated attempts by the federal government to deploy the military to restore order in cities like Los Angeles, Seattle, and New York were met not only with civil disobedience and insurrection, but ultimately by armed resistance from the so-called 'National Guard' and police forces of these cities and states, under orders from Governors and Mayors opposed to the President. By 2040, this constitutional crisis ended with the secession of the California Republic, the Republic of Cascadia (Oregon and Washington), Gotham (New York and New Jersey), and New England from the Former United States. This also meant that by 2042 what was left of the USA redefined itself as a resurgence of the Confederate States of America, with the star-studded and blue crossed flaming red rebel banner of Dixie as its flag. Texas, which briefly flirted with a declaration of independence, decided to become the economic backbone of the CSA rather than to go it alone. People in the more liberal parts of Colorado, the Midwest, and Louisiana who resisted this *democratically* resurgent Confederacy, were crushed by the rightwing white majority who had by now seen liberal and diverse parts of the Former USA turn into the equivalent of failed states and banana republics worse than Detroit.

The United Nations, which, after the devastation of New York City, had relocated its headquarters to the Palais de Nations in Geneva, could do little to stop the CSA from forming a transatlantic alliance with those parts of Europe turning hard to the Right in the name of preserving the values, heritage, and ethnic identity of Faustian Civilization. This "Atlantic Alliance", a rightist reimagining of NATO, also included Argentina and was looking to expand into the whiter parts of Latin America.

Such was the situation around 2045 when, after years of precipitous sea-level rise from the secretly engineered meltdown in Greenland and Antarctica, the North Atlantic Current failed, plunging Northwestern Europe and the upper half of North America into barely survivable glacial conditions. A mass evacuation of Northern and Western Europe was organized by the Atlantic Alliance, which was effectively a public relations apparatus for the Spider. Only those Europeans with the right sociopolitical outlook and ideology were allowed to immediately immigrate to the Confederate States of America and to Argentina. As they became entrenched in their new home, they also Europeanized its social character, high culture, and style of governance. Hardy libertarian frontiersmen from the northern states of the Confederacy were also able to resettle further to the south. However, when desperate people from the liberal 'multi-cultural' states of New England, New York, and New Jersey that had seceded from the Former USA pleaded to be repatriated as "Americans" they were slaughtered as they illegally crossed the northeastern border of the Confederacy.

It is into such a world that the White Devils came – and conquered, when they declared themselves openly in 2048. To the vast majority of survivors in the Faustian World these superhuman Nordics of an "elder race" appeared to be saviors, even angels. Just before the failure of the North Atlantic current, enough of the ice had melted in Antarctica that the ruins of Atlantis were discovered by corporatists attempting to exploit the thawing continent for its formerly inaccessible oil resources. As the gargantuan high-precision stone structures in New Swabia began to be surveyed, the surviving Atlanteans disclosed their presence and claimed the excavated cities as their homeland. When their extensive presence on the Moon and Mars was also revealed, all but the most Promethean souls were awed into submission and surrendered to the desire to be "saved."

OTHER BOOKS PUBLISHED BY ARKTOS

SRI DHARMA PRAVARTAKA ACHARYA · *The Dharma Manifesto*

JOAKIM ANDERSEN · *Rising from the Ruins: The Right of the 21st Century*

WINSTON C. BANKS · *Excessive Immigration*

ALAIN DE BENOIST · *Beyond Human Rights*
Carl Schmitt Today
The Indo-Europeans
Manifesto for a European Renaissance
On the Brink of the Abyss
The Problem of Democracy
Runes and the Origins of Writing
View from the Right (vol. 1–3)

ARTHUR MOELLER VAN DEN BRUCK · *Germany's Third Empire*

MATT BATTAGLIOLI · *The Consequences of Equality*

KERRY BOLTON · *Revolution from Above*
Yockey: A Fascist Odyssey

ISAC BOMAN · *Money Power*

RICARDO DUCHESNE · *Faustian Man in a Multicultural Age*

ALEXANDER DUGIN · *Ethnos and Society*
Ethnosociology
Eurasian Mission
The Fourth Political Theory
Last War of the World-Island
Political Platonism
Putin vs Putin
The Rise of the Fourth Political Theory

EDWARD DUTTON · *Race Differences in Ethnocentrism*

MARK DYAL · *Hated and Proud*

CLARE ELLIS · *The Blackening of Europe*

KOENRAAD ELST · *Return of the Swastika*

JULIUS EVOLA · *The Bow and the Club*
Fascism Viewed from the Right
A Handbook for Right-Wing Youth
Metaphysics of War
The Myth of the Blood
Notes on the Third Reich

	The Path of Cinnabar *Recognitions* *A Traditionalist Confronts Fascism*
GUILLAUME FAYE	*Archeofuturism* *Archeofuturism 2.0* *The Colonisation of Europe* *Convergence of Catastrophes* *Ethnic Apocalypse* *A Global Coup* *Sex and Deviance* *Understanding Islam* *Why We Fight*
DANIEL S. FORREST	*Suprahumanism*
ANDREW FRASER	*Dissident Dispatches* *The WASP Question*
GÉNÉRATION IDENTITAIRE	*We are Generation Identity*
PETER GOODCHILD	*The Taxi Driver from Baghdad*
PAUL GOTTFRIED	*War and Democracy*
PORUS HOMI HAVEWALA	*The Saga of the Aryan Race*
LARS HOLGER HOLM	*Hiding in Broad Daylight* *Homo Maximus* *Incidents of Travel in Latin America* *The Owls of Afrasiab*
RICHARD HOUCK	*Liberalism Unmasked*
A. J. ILLINGWORTH	*Political Justice*
ALEXANDER JACOB	*De Naturae Natura*
JASON REZA JORJANI	*Iranian Leviathan* *Lovers of Sophia* *Novel Folklore* *Prometheism* *Prometheus and Atlas* *World State of Emergency*
HENRIK JONASSON	*Sigmund*
VINCENT JOYCE	*The Long Goodbye*
RODERICK KAINE	*Smart and SeXy*

OTHER BOOKS PUBLISHED BY ARKTOS

OTHER BOOKS PUBLISHED BY ARKTOS

Made in the USA
Las Vegas, NV
11 October 2023

78941590R00111